INSIDE THE WHALE

Inside the Whale

Jennie Rooney

Chatto & Windus
LONDON

Published by Chatto & Windus 2008

2 4 6 8 10 9 7 5 3 1

First published in Great Britain in 2008 by
Chatto & Windus
Random House, 20 Vauxhall Bridge Road,
London SW1V 2SA

www.rbooks.co.uk

Addresses for companies within The Random House Group Limited
can be found at:
www.randomhouse.co.uk/offices.htm

The Random House Group Limited Reg. No. 954009

A CIP catalogue record for this book
is available from the British Library

Trade paperback ISBN 9780701185411

The Random House Group Limited supports The Forest Stewardship Council (FSC),
the leading international forest certification organisation. All our titles that are
printed on Greenpeace approved FSC certified paper carry the FSC logo. Our paper
procurement policy can be found at www.rbooks.co.uk/environment

Mixed Sources
Product group from well-managed
forests and other controlled sources
www.fsc.org Cert no. TT-COC-2139
© 1996 Forest Stewardship Council
FSC

Typeset in Palatino by Palimpsest Book Production Ltd,
Grangemouth, Stirlingshire

Printed and bound in Great Britain by
CPI Mackays, Chatham ME5 8TD

For my brothers, that they may be devoured whole;
and also for Frank.

Now the Lord had prepared a great fish to swallow up Jonah. And Jonah was in the belly of the fish for three days and three nights.

Then Jonah prayed unto the Lord his God out of the fish's belly . . .

And the Lord spake unto the fish, and it vomited out Jonah upon the dry land.

Book of Jonah 1:17, 2:1, 2:10

Stevie

My mum was in her element during that hot September of 1939.

Over the years, she had developed a nervous streak. We became accustomed to hearing her mutter about the dangers of the motor car as she chopped onions. She fretted about untied shoelaces and ribbons on cardigan sleeves. She baulked at ponytails that could be yanked by any passing madman, and wrote letters to *The Times* about the perils of air travel, citing the misfortunes of a distant cousin who had been blown off course at the opening of the Greenwich Railway in a hot-air balloon and had crash-landed on the railway arches at London Bridge. She believed that any child who had the misfortune to place so much as a slice of cucumber in its mouth after having retrieved it from the floor would face an imminent and almost certain death.

Birthdays were particularly dangerous occasions as far as my mum, Vivien, was concerned. The very idea of carrying a cake bursting with naked flames into a darkened room made her left eye twitch. Vivien would lay a small bowl of water next to each person's plate which we all had to clasp as the cake entered the room, our knees bent in readiness to extinguish the flames at the first sign of unruliness among the candles.

We woke up early on the first Sunday of September that year, and it felt like Christmas Day. My brothers put on their school uniforms for church, and left them on all day because everybody knew that if there was going to be a war, it was going to start then, and they wanted to be ready for it. I was wearing a pair of scrubbed white gloves that were reserved for special occasions and a navy blue pinafore that was getting rather too tight around the bust to be altogether seemly.

The war was announced at eleven o'clock. We were all in Mrs Bartram's yard at Number 10, listening to Chamberlain on the wireless that she had balanced precariously next to a dead bee on the kitchen windowsill. Number 7 were there too. I picked up Mrs Bartram's cat and ran my hand up its back towards its head. It growled at me as Chamberlain announced that we were at war and I noticed that the inside of its mouth was a surprisingly fierce shade of red.

I spent the afternoon with my younger brothers, Eddy and George, filling bags with government sand that had been left at the end of our road. At first we tried to be solemn, but the sand stayed between our toes and settled into the cracks of our hands and the bags ended up bulging with turreted sandcastles and small sculptures of domestic animals.

Meanwhile, our house was slowly filling up with water. Vivien was gleefully hiding brimming bowls under the settee and balancing full glass bottles next to our beds. She left heavy long-handled pans to ripple excitedly on the sideboard in the front room and hung

2

rugs over the doors to allow for the quick smothering of fires. She lined the edges of the windows with putty and stuffed the chimney with newspaper. She placed a pile of neatly folded damp flannels on the mantelpiece in case of a sudden gas attack on the front room.

It was generally assumed, although never openly admitted, that if any part of the house were going to be invaded, it would undoubtedly be the front room. It had the nice curtains, after all. We lined the sandbags along the front wall in keeping with this accepted proposition and piled tins of condensed milk under the table in case of a siege. We planted cress in old cigarette tins and placed them on the windowsill, to prevent scurvy.

Vivien sighed happily as she looked around at all the precautions she was now allowed, if not obliged, to take. She slept more deeply that night than I had ever known, her hair splayed dramatically over the pillow and her arms hanging carelessly from the sides of the bed, snoring softly.

So that is how I remember the beginning of the war. Wet flannels and sand, and cress growing from damp cotton wool folded flatly in tins. There were no maps spread across the kitchen table, no series of small swastikas marking Hitler's progress through the smaller countries of Europe, like in the history books that came after. There was no talk in our yard of concentration camps or of the rise of European dictatorship or of German economic stagnation. I know all that now, but it has been added later, laid gently over the bits I remember, like tracing paper.

And that is the problem with the beginnings of things.

Michael

It is a strange thing, sleeping with morphine. It rocks you, gathers you into its dark arms, and slithers with you over the surface of sleep. It softens nightmares like bathwater, and dulls the crashing, skidding pain in my throat. In the mornings I feel it pricking the edges of my skin, nestling in the cracks of my elbows and along my spine. It leaves my mind empty, alert. In the mornings, I remember everything.

I remember sequences of kings and queens, and the order of stations on the Northern Line, both branches. I remember Darwin's lists of sub-races of pigeons, and how to tell a gurney from a logan. And I remember the long stories that Brendan Hardcastle used to tell me after school when we sat with swinging legs on the high wall that ran along the back of our yards, for Brendan always knew everything before I did.

It was Brendan who first told me about Mr Samuel Finley Breese Morse. He told me that, in 1844, Sam Morse attended the first public exhibition of his newly invented code. The display was held in the chamber of the Supreme Court of the United States of America in Washington. A young lady came forward and selected the words that Sam Morse was to send to his associate

4

in Baltimore. She laid a piece of paper on the table in front of him, and the first message ever to be transmitted via an insulated electromagnetic wire was tapped out in full view of the US Commissioner of Patents, the young lady's father.

The message arrived in Baltimore and was sent back over the same wire, and both times it asked the same question: *What hath God wrought?*

Twice transmitted, twice greeted with gasps, and twice left hanging, unanswered and ignorant of its own magnitude. After all, the twentieth century was not yet so much as a glint in the eye of the 1800s and that young lady could not possibly have known what the twentieth century would bring for two small boys swinging their legs over a back wall in 1931.

But what Brendan could not yet tell me was that ninety-seven years after that first message was sent, at the age of twenty and with a dent of forty-one years already blown into the sides of the new century, we would be wedging our knees into the dusty cracks of the Abyssinian desert and flattening our Royal Signals hats against our chests as Alf's body was lowered into the ground. He could not tell me that when he turned his burnt neck to look at me that day I would not be able to hold his eyes, and that as I lay awake in bed that night I would remember the young lady in the chamber of the Supreme Court and I would think to myself, *What indeed?*

In the mornings, mostly, I remember that.

Stevie

I'll try again.

I was born in 1924. I gave birth in 1941. I married in 1945. A thin discrepancy, but an obvious one, like the gap between a pair of front teeth.

After I left school, I spent four years chopping root vegetables in the canteen of the Sun Pat peanut factory on the Old Kent Road. I had wanted to be a teacher with a high collar and a bag for my books with a clasp that snapped shut, but instead I found myself arranging pale cabbages on trays and chopping carrots into perfect cubes. They made me stand on a wooden box so that my elbows didn't disturb the other women.

But already I am skipping things. That is not the absolute beginning. I need to be more thorough.

I was originally named as a question, my first two names being scratched drippily onto my birth certificate in reverse. May Stephanie Ponder? The nurse tutted at Vivien, plunging me in cold water as she warned that no child with a question mark at the end of its name would ever be able to sleep. Night or day. Vivien took me home and I lay wide-eyed in my cot, wrapped in blue cotton with white edges, unable even to blink. She had to dab my eyes with spittle on a ball of cotton wool to stop them from drying out completely.

Five months later I was crossed out and re-entered into the parish register, this time as a permission, and a possibility. Stephanie May Ponder. The vicar nodded his head sagely and pressed his thumb into the dip above my nose for a second time and I slept for two days.

Vivien was employed by a local property solicitor to copy out deeds in immaculate copperplate onto thick yellow paper. She did this at the kitchen table, lining her pen nibs up in front of the salt and pepper and spreading her fingers defensively when we came too close to the inkpot. In the evenings, she sat in the chair next to the fire and sewed box pleats into pastel-coloured skirts and realigned the hems of flat-fronted trousers. She hung the finished garments along the curtain rail in her bedroom where they flapped against the glass like prisoners until they were collected.

My dad worked as a tube driver for London Transport, leaving the house noisily before dawn and returning in the afternoon with dry eyes and swept-back hair. A soft breeze would rattle the window in its pane as he approached, and Vivien would purse her lips and dutifully remove the net from her hair. When the government announced its plan to turn the Metropolitan Line into a circle, the thought of it was too much for my dad to bear. He lay down in the front room with a loud sigh and announced that enough was enough.

After that, he spent a lot of time lying in the crack between the crumb-coloured cushions on the settee. He smelt of old books with crackly pages. Sometimes we didn't see him for weeks. We lived around the settee but not on it. He would come back to us by blinking loudly without warning, gasping for air, and we would look at him in surprise, wrinkling our noses as if he were a forgotten sandwich with dry curling corners and brown lettuce.

He didn't seem to notice the others. His arm would reach out, beckoning me closer, ignoring my sister and my brothers who were busily pattering sideways out of the door, trying to avoid the creaky floorboard. His hand would clamp around my wrist and he would ask me questions, small and round questions that shone like lost pennies as he held them out to me. It was our only form of communication.

The questions became more specialised as the months went on. At first, they took general, primary themes. Capital cities of Europe, prime number sequences, spellings with silent Gs lurking at the edges. I graduated to the capital cities of Asia on the day my teacher called me to the front of the class to announce that I was going to Houghton Hall in North Dulwich because I had won a scholarship and that everyone had to clap and call me Stephanie from now on because Stevie was no name for a girl in a boater hat.

My dad questioned me on the inner workings of electro-magnetic induction rings on the day my first period came and I cried because I didn't know the answer. I didn't usually cry. And then there were conjugations in Latin that I practised at school and carried home carefully in mauve exercise books to show him.

I had to learn poems and recite them to him with feeling. My dad did not like to be looked at during poems. So instead I would stand at the window and shout 'Sea Fever' at passers-by with my scholarship-white gloves clasped in front of me, and my dad would shut his eyes and smile and then roll back into the crack between the settee and the cushions and I would be dismissed.

The day before he died, he asked me if I knew the square root of minus two.

I told him that there wasn't one.

It became the last thing I ever said to him, and it was only as the coffin was lowered into the ground and I heard Vivien breathe out completely for the first time in ten years that I realised I had questions of my own I had never dared to ask.

It was arranged that I was to leave Houghton Hall after that. On 21 October 1937, which was a Thursday, I exchanged my white cotton gloves with satin buttons for blue factory ones, packed my newly-found vowel sounds into my pencil case along with my Latin verbs, and zipped it tightly shut as I walked from the gates.

I met Michael a week later. I can picture his face as if it were right there in front of me. Not as he was when I last saw him. When I think of Michael, it is as he was when he was a boy, at the beginning of everything.

Before he disappeared.

But I must try harder to remember the other things. After all, *his* is not the face I want to remember.

Michael

I dream of the Sorrowful Mysteries. I count them in my head, up to five, my fingers gripping the beads of my rosary as I sleep. *My God, My God, why have you forsaken me?* I wake up suddenly, always at the same point, my throat too large for my neck. *I thirst.* I tilt my head and look around, groping for my glasses. I lift them to my eyes and, just for a second, in the half-light of my empty bedroom, I see Alf slumped faintly against the wall, next to the fireplace.

Is that delusional?

My brother, Ben, was three years older than me and I thought he was the funniest person in the whole world. He once told me that our father's Great-Great-Great-Uncle James had tried to shoot King George III in an attempt to hasten the Second Coming of Christ. Apparently, it was thought that one event would precipitate the other, although the exact details of the causative link remained opaque. Our father did not like to be reminded of this particular relative. He felt it reflected badly on him.

My father owned a small urban dairy in the Borough, and we lived in the rooms above the shop. He was a very precise man, tall and silvery with huge arms that looked as though they might be comforting to be held in, and a long stretch in his fingers. He synchronised all the clocks in the house every morning and sent blank postcards to himself once a week, telling us that someone had to keep an eye on the efficiency of the postal service. He stirred his tea with a thermometer, and kept a meticulous record of the milk output of our four cows.

Ben and I were terrified of him. It surprised me, when I thought of it years later, that he had ever told Ben about his Great-Great-Great-Uncle James. In general, my father never spoke of his childhood and I only knew that he did not start life as a grown man because my mother told me. She also told me that he had been sent to the seminary at the age of eleven because his parents could not afford to keep him, and so I should feel sorry for him. My father was the eldest of eight brothers, and his mother, my grandmother, eventually died in child-birth while producing the daughter for whom she had feverishly prayed. The Jesuits taught my father that his mother's death was a punishment from God for her covetousness and my father did not ever quite manage to fully dismiss this reasoning. Given the nature of his occupation, such disregard for the germ theory of infection was worrying.

He was a difficult man to feel sorry for.

But the point is this. The court decided that my father's Great-Great-Great-Uncle James, when attempting to shoot the king as he applauded from the Royal Box at the Theatre Royal in Drury Lane, was suffering from a state of delusion at the time he pulled the trigger. He

11

was found guilty by reason of insanity and locked up indefinitely.

That is what I am getting at.

I roll this thought around my head for a moment and then I lean over to switch on the light. I check my watch. She will be leaving her house soon. I take a mouthful of tea from the Thermos next to my bed and it explodes out of me in a dramatic fit of hiccups. There is an immovable lump where my oesophagus should be and my pyjamas are spotted with tepid milky tea. I enjoy the warmth as it soaks through the stripy cotton of what I once thought was a distinguished Dickensian nightshirt, and I shut my eyes and imagine her face once more. Of course, she does not look like that anymore. She is old now and pulls her shopping behind her in a brown trolley bag and she no longer recognises me. When I see her she looks back at me, but she just sees a man who can hardly stand up straight, wrapped all in wool.

I should probably explain something. The doctor came to my house this morning. She wanted to give me more details, read leaflets to me, update me on medical developments. She leant across me, saying my name over and over again until I began to wince at the sound of it. I kept my eyes shut. I was not ready for the specifics. I didn't want names and time frames. She scrabbled about for my wrist and took my pulse, and eventually she went away to phone for an ambulance to take me to the hospital. I sat up abruptly in my bed and told the doctor that I would come in tomorrow, for good. Because once I am in, there is only one way out.

And I just need a little more time.

Stevie

I have discovered that if I approach my ear from a certain angle, I can slot a pound coin into the cavity and wedge it there. It stays quite easily, held in by those little lumps that jut out just above the earlobe. Even when I tilt my head and shake it a little, the pound coin does not budge. It is a pleasing discovery.

I like the way it glints underneath my hair. Jonathan hated my hair when it was this short. It bristled around my forehead and ended abruptly at the nape of my neck. It made him sneeze in the night when I burrowed sleepily into him. He would push me away, rolling me to the edge of the bed like a discarded newspaper, and my ankles would catch in the sheets and pull them tightly across his legs. I would wake up in disgrace, clawing the edge of the bed.

I let my hair grow when he got ill so that he would let me sleep next to him. The house smelt of cut knees and antiseptic wipes. My hair drooped over my ears like a fried egg. It got into my eyes and distracted people from looking too closely when they asked after Jonathan. It relieved the urge I had to drag those people by the lower forearm into our house and say, *this is how he's doing, what did you expect? And by the way, can you smell anything funny?*

I had it cut short again after the funeral last week. The woman at the till pressed a small tub of orange paste into my hand as I left, as a tester, she said, to make my hair look more styled. I replied politely that it was just what I needed. It is sitting on the bookshelf. It makes me a little nervous. I can't remember what I am supposed to do with it, whether I should put it on when my hair is wet or dry or somewhere in between, and how much I should use. There is an ambiguous label on the back that I read through a magnifying glass which claims it is suitable for application at all times, but I am suspicious of such a statement. One time must be better than another and, now that I am seventy-five, it is too late to experiment. So I shall leave it where it is. I have no need for styled hair.

I remove the pound coin from my ear and slip it into my pocket, and then I open the front door. As I approach the bus stop, I see that the old man is back. He is slumped against the red plastic bench, his face distorted by his thick glasses and half-hidden behind a grey scarf. His presence unnerves me and yet I am almost relieved to see him. He hasn't been there for weeks. He watches me climb onto the bus and this time I nod to him as it pulls away. He lifts his hand to his mouth and I almost think he might be waving at me. Without thinking, I raise my hand to the window as the bus turns the corner, and I see him struggle to his feet.

The journey to the library exhausts me. I feel it now in my knees and in the joints of my fingers. I sit at the table with my pile of books while the late autumn sun pushes brightly against the glass of the window. The air above my head is heavy with motes. I am still only at

G of the large-print fiction section. I have nineteen more letters to get through before I can stop.

The librarian looks at me as I settle into my chair. She is too young to understand my fundamental need for alphabetical order and time consumption. She thinks I am merely pedantic, but she cannot know how it feels. After all, what else is there for me to do? Watch daytime television? Write another letter to the Prime Minister? I'm tired of all that. I lift my arm and swipe the shiny jacket flaps of *Brighton Rock* at the flecks of dust above my head, and I watch them scatter and spin.

Michael

I have lost the ability to speak. They have told me there is an operation they could do but they are stalling, for obvious reasons. I don't really mind. After all, I can clap my hands, click my fingers, push the button next to my bed, fart both involuntarily and on demand, tap my pen on my headboard, whistle. I wonder if it will be enough.

You see, what the doctors don't tell you is this. The human ear is not an expansive organ. It allows us only a sliver of the full acoustic spectrum. What sounds like the deepest silence is in fact a cacophony of sound, a melee of screaming meteors, of roaring drizzle and howling clouds, accompanied by an incessant low hum coming from the centre of the earth.

And they don't mention that the sounds we do hear are nothing more than fast-decaying vibrations of material that lose energy almost immediately, fading away while we try desperately to rearrange the vibrations into something more meaningful. And yet, the sporadic production of audible mid-range waves is expected of us. It is the only way, so we are told, of connecting with others, of expressing emotions, of passing the time.

Click.

I wake with a start. A nurse, introduced to me yesterday as Doreen, huffs crossly as she pulls at the blinds, her pink arm wobbling heavily with the effort.

'Come on,' she bleats. 'Rise and shine.' She lifts my head with a jerk and pushes my chin onto my neck as she wedges a pillow behind me. Her breath is milky on my neck and I try to wipe it off with my hand. It smudges and stays there, moist and scaly.

'There, that's better,' she shouts unconvincingly into my ear. I flinch at the volume. She stretches the sheets over me, retucking them at the corners so that I am wedged flat. I reach for the pad of paper that hangs from a string next to my bed but I cannot turn far enough to reach it. I am trapped.

Click.

I jump again. Doreen has turned the light off once more and is squinting at the damp sky. 'It's quite dark out there this morning.' She glares at me. 'Shall I leave the light on?' She reaches a chubby finger to the switch and I realise it is not a question.

Click.

I flinch.

She looks at me. 'You want it off?' she barks. *Click.*

I shake my head.

'I wish you'd make up your mind,' she mutters.

Click.

We force smiles at each other and she leaves me squinting at the light. I try to work my feet loose from where the sheet is flattening them.

Click. The light is switched on in the cubicle next to me. And so it begins again.

My enforced silence does not alarm me. After all, I am

used to silence. My generation was not renowned for its loquacity when faced with screaming shells and creeping U-boats. We went silently, patriotism obsolete and faintly ridiculous by 1939. Nobody believed in it the second time around. Not twice in a lifetime.

We went in silence and we returned in silence. The sounds we made were outside the audible limits of human hearing. The ultrasonic waves that came from the savage madnesses of the second war were too high to be heard without the use of sophisticated aneroid micro-barometers. It was a new and crazy form of war that took the spectators by surprise. The frequency of sound emitted by hurtling Japanese kamikaze was measured at several megahertz; the high hiss of the gas chambers was too far above the human auditory threshold of 20,000 hertz to be properly absorbed. All of it was incomprehensible without a filter.

And then there were the other sounds, the sounds that came after, human sounds. Long deep moans at frequencies so low they could only be heard by elephants and whales.

So, to the human ear, it all sounded like silence.

Click. Doreen has moved to the next cubicle.

At the beginning of the war, when I was posted on the radio network with Alf in North Africa, we had to issue instructions to moving tanks, tracking them down and trying to keep a record of their positions in the Somali deserts. We would follow them on our radios, talking to them, growing accustomed to their habits and their voices. But there was something we knew which we did not tell them. We knew that eventually, inevitably, in the middle of a word, there would come a click over the radio, as soft as a light switch. And then silence.

Alf could not cope with the clicks. He would get up and punch and scratch at the walls, scraping the skin from his knuckles. 'They've got another one. The fuckers have got another one.' He would hiss the words through his teeth, his dark eyes shiny and wet, sweat running down his face next to his ears.

There was nothing I could say. I would change frequency and wait for a new connection while Alf rocked behind me, his head resting against the back of my chair. And later I would send in a report, mentioning that a tank had been hit, translating the incident into the dots and dashes of Morse so that I no longer had to think about it in words, avoiding Alf's eye. He was just a boy after all. I thought I was protecting him.

But I was just a boy too. Who was I to think I could look after him?

Doreen's head appears around my curtain. 'Breakfast!' she hollers, the word vibrating around the very centre of the standard audible range. I smile faintly, waiting for the waves of sound to subside, and I wonder when Anna's shift will begin.

Stevie

We held the funeral at St Andrew's. St Andrew's is one of those modern churches, with green carpets and white walls and a smell of post-Reformation cleaning products. I would have liked somewhere a bit grander, besteepled with soaring stone and reeking of incense, but the others were either booked up or had difficult vicars.

Everyone kept looking at me. I wasn't sure what was going on and was finding it difficult to remember why I was there at all. I kept quiet and sat at the front and tried to think about sad things to make myself cry. Dog bites and bee stings. I felt the tears beginning to prick the edges of my eyelashes.

Emily, my daughter, was at the lectern, talking into a microphone. Her voice was too loud and it echoed off the whiteness of the walls so that I couldn't tell when one word became another. She seemed to be humming in B flat. I concentrated on looking straight ahead. The buttons of her cardigan were done up wrongly, and her lipstick was too bright. It washed her out. She always wore lipstick that was too bright and I was just thinking that it had been a while since I had mentioned the subject of her lipstick when she stopped speaking suddenly.

Everyone was looking at me with tilted heads. I kept my eyes on Emily, watching her as she stepped down from the pulpit and padded quietly along the green carpet and sat down next to me again. I noticed the coffin and the photograph of Jonathan that Anna, my grand-daughter, had propped against its side – and suddenly I remembered. I wanted to leave. I didn't believe in any of this. It would make no difference, and pretending that it did seemed suddenly ridiculous and tiring.

I went to see the vicar after the service. I found him in the vestry, standing in front of an old chest of drawers, dressed all in white. The green cloth that he wore around his neck during the service was folded clumsily on a chair. He was running a comb through the few remaining strands of hair on his scalp, parting them at the side and dabbing them flat with his fingers.

I coughed as I stepped into the room and he jumped slightly, hurriedly slipping the comb into a drawer and arranging things around it.

'Thank you, Vicar,' I said. 'The ceremony was nice. Just right, I think.'

'I'm glad.' He paused and we looked at each other for a while. Eventually he said, 'I thought Emily's speech was very touching.'

'Yes,' I replied absently.

A beam of light fell onto the top of the vicar's head from the tiny square window high up in the wall. He bit the edge of his nail and said, 'We had better go outside. Everyone will be waiting for us.'

'Vicar,' I hesitated. 'I'm scared for him.'

He looked at me. 'Your husband was a good man. God will take care of him.' He pressed his hands together as

21

if in prayer, and then looked up quickly and handed me a chocolate bar.

I nodded uncertainly, taking the chocolate and noticing how the paint on the wall behind him was peeling off in huge curls. The vicar picked up the green cloth and we walked outside together.

We joined the crowd that had gathered in the car park of the church. I stood there, clutching my chocolate bar, and suddenly I realised that I had forgotten to buy any pickled onions. It was the only thing Emily had asked me to do and I had forgotten. I nudged the vicar conspiratorially.

'I don't suppose you have any pickled onions at home, do you?' I whispered.

'Of course.'

'Might I borrow them?' I asked and then added, by way of clarification, 'For the finger buffet.'

He nodded jovially, in a manner that suggested he understood that a finger buffet would not be complete without a selection of pickled vegetables. 'You can have them.'

'Thank you,' I whispered.

The funeral cars were dark and heavy. The driver was singing along to the radio in a voice that was too high for his shaven head and rounded shoulders when Anna opened the door of the car for me. He coughed abruptly at the interruption and turned off the music as we shuffled into the back seat. We drove in silence, disturbed only by the prim ticking of the indicator.

Everyone else was already there by the time we arrived. The cemetery wafted with newly planted trees. Anna waited in the car. I wanted to wait there too, but Emily had already taken my arm and was dragging me along the gravel path towards the plot we had reserved. It was nearly over. I was relieved. Perhaps I should have specified that I wanted silverskin onions, not just normal pickled ones. I looked up at the vicar and wondered which sort he would go for. He winked at me as he gestured to the pall-bearers, and I thought he probably went for silverskin.

I held onto Emily's arm and tried to think of nothing at all. The late afternoon sky swelled at the edges like a purple grape as the coffin was lowered into the ground. I bent down to pick up a handful of dust and, as I did, I thought of the photograph in the church. I saw the dates Anna had scrawled across the bottom of it: 1919–1998. I remembered the shape of my husband's body, the outline of his head, the red scarf he was wearing on the day the photograph was taken.

And suddenly I began to cry, because I could not see his face.

Michael

I have forgotten how to sleep. Insomnia has implanted itself coldly on my nose and sapped the blood from my feet. I feel it pressing into my spine like a frozen pea, hidden under the disinfected hospital mattress. I need more morphine.

I try tapping out the lists my father taught me as a child onto the table next to my bed. I find this helps me to relax. I am comforted by their predictability, their rhythm, although their substance terrifies me still. They block and remind in equal measure.

There is one list that swamps all others, a list of the things my father told me would send me straight to Hell.

Permitting Injustice to the Wage Earner
Sodomy
Stealing Large Things
Fornication
Oppressing the Poor
Murder
Missing Mass on Sundays and Holy Days of Obligation
Disobedience

24

My father taught me this list when I was six years old. These were his favourites among the recognised sins. These were the ones he graced with Germanic capital letters. This was his extended version of the Sins that Cried to Heaven for Vengeance. I slip the ones I have committed nonchalantly among the others, hoping they won't be noticed.

The latter two items on the list made my mother roll her eyeballs under her eyelids so that you were never quite sure if you had seen them roll or not. I tried stealing this gesture for myself and repeating it subversively at school in an attempt at garnering admiration from the other boys. They did not bat so much as a stubby eyelash at me. I caught their attention only briefly during catechism instruction when I thrust my hand into the air to enquire if Sodomy was worse than swearing. I had no conception of my crime, being ignorant as to the physical manifestations of half of the Sins that Cried to Heaven until I learnt the whispered explanations of these words in the playground at secondary school. Until then, I had lived in fear of inadvertent Fornication and there was no one I could ask to clarify what it might be in order that I might avoid it.

I was hauled by my ear out of the classroom and presented to the headmaster as a singularly vulgar boy, an accusation that was marked upon me in garish red stripes on the backs of my pale legs, and was not quite in keeping with my otherwise sombre school attire. I had to slope against walls for a week until the marks had gone, rupturing my elbows with splinters, in case a confession was wrought from me over the dinner table and Singular Vulgarity added to the list.

I was, on the whole, a nervous child.

From an early age, I was exposed to an unusually cold version of the life yet to come. It would be sprayed over us at mealtimes so that by the time we picked up our cutlery we would be glistening like chipped icicles. There were no blistering flames to offer even a faint hope of warmth in the second before they consumed. My father's vision was pure ice. It was made from words that tumbled in sculpted shards from his mouth and shattered on the plate in front of him. Our food was always cold by the time we were allowed to eat it.

My mother would sit with her head lowered, tracing the patterns in the woven tablemats with her eyes and rubbing her hands to keep warm. Ben and I watched our father's long fingers curl as he spoke, softly thumping the table to keep time to his words. The knives and forks would jump to attention and I would feel my stomach rumble.

When he finally ran out of words, he would sit down, red in the face and exhausted, letting the silence ring in our ears. Ben would look at me and raise his eyebrows.

'Water, Mother? Michael?' he would ask, lifting the jug of water from the middle of the table and holding it too high over our beakers. He would tilt it until the water fell noisily and rudely onto the ceramic, like a boy pissing into a bowl, and I had to cover my mouth with my hand to stifle my giggles. Ben always kept his mouth ironed straight as he poured the water but the sides of his eyes would crease almost imperceptibly as he looked at me, and my father would click his tongue crossly and tell me to try to contain myself.

Hell was an ever-present fear in my childhood. It flickered disconcertingly in mirrors and shop windows, plaguing me in the way that other small boys were plagued by oversized ears and double crowns. I had no distinguishing features to distract myself from these images. I was quite unremarkable. In his softer moments, my father would ruffle my hair and tell me that one day I would make the perfect spy, and I would beam with pleasure. It was only as I grew older that I realised this was not intended as a compliment. The Hell that I saw in windows was a cold, green place inhabited by gnarled, frostbitten fingers and fantastically long, dripping noses. It was a place that bore no relation to my existence, and yet was never far from my consciousness. I thought it was a habit I would grow out of.

I did grow out of Hell for a while when I met Stevie, and the prospect of eternal damnation became less of a priority. Sunday mornings niggled at me like minor infidelities, drunken half-kisses left unconsummated, but nothing more than that. I was distracted by the softness of her lips and the way she reached distractedly for my hand as she walked, not even looking at me, and I would allow myself to push the thought of it out of my head.

It was only a temporary reprise. Hell came back to me with a violence I was not quite ready for in a malaria ward in Addis Ababa. It landed in my stomach like a clenched fist, winding me, bending me double as I held Alf's body in my bloodstained hands and I realised that I had forgotten to be afraid, and it was this my father had been trying to warn me against.

I roll onto my side and press my face into the pillow, trying to stop the chattering in my teeth. Already it is so cold.

I have considered the possibility of asking for a priest but I am uncertain of the ethics pertaining to late confessions. It doesn't seem fair to allow it. After all, there is something morally reprehensible about goal-hanging. I imagine there is a medieval version of the offside rule preventing last-minute sacramental reconciliation.

The doctor in the hospital tells me quietly that it is only a matter of weeks. I think she is being optimistic. It is only polite, after all, in her line of work.

So don't get me wrong. This is not a confession. I don't believe in confessions. And anyway, it is too late to start now. It would take too long.

But all the same, perhaps I will tell Anna, now that I am here.

Stevie

I have a pathological fear of the barriers at tube stations closing on me. I think the probability of it actually happening must increase each time I get through unscathed and it makes me nervous. I hope Anna hasn't noticed. It is embarrassing being old in front of the young.

I hold my breath as we go through the barriers at Greenwich. The air in the park tastes metallic and shiny and the grass breaks off in icy stalks as we walk. We sit on a bench next to the lake and I get tangled up in an unwieldy section of newspaper.

'Are you okay?' Anna asks.

I nod. 'There are no boats on the lake. There were always boats here before.'

'They've probably put them away for the winter,' she says.

'It's only the beginning of September,' I tut irritably.

Anna takes my arm and holds it tightly, smiling at me. 'It's November, Nana.'

'Oh.' My breath comes out in a cloud and I watch it, surprised.

There are children hanging from the sundial in front of us. Anna is talking to me but I cannot focus on her words. Perhaps I am too easily distracted. This park is a little too much for me.

'Don't you think that's a bit weird?' she asks, suddenly animated.

'What is?'

'Kate's sister is having the *Jaws* theme tune playing when she walks up the aisle at her wedding. Have you not been listening?'

'I'm sorry,' I say. 'Of course I've been listening. But I don't know what the *Jaws* theme tune sounds like.' It suddenly seems the saddest thing in the world, not to know the *Jaws* theme tune.

She rolls her eyes, and then takes off her scarf and wraps it gently around my neck. 'What's the matter, Nana?'

'This park. I haven't been here since I was a girl. I used to come all the time.'

'With Granddad?'

'No. With someone else.'

She doesn't ask. I don't tell her. It is my secret and it is something I like to forget. I have bundled up my memories of those years before I met Jonathan, wrapped them in brown paper with dented corners and white string and buried them in a dark corner. But occasionally things come to me in the night. They elbow their way into my dreams and rumple my sheets and make my pillow too hot.

Of course, most of the time I'm fine. I smile absently at small children. I let other people onto the bus ahead of me. I ask shopkeepers personal questions as I wait for my change. But recently, since the funeral, I have been allowing my thoughts to wander. I have been letting my eyes linger too long on curly-haired young men with square backs and strong jawlines. It makes me dizzy. I have to sit down and make myself forget again before I can go on with whatever I was doing. Or have a camomile tea.

It is a difficult time, the doctor says, the first few months.

Michael and I came here one Sunday afternoon, before the war. We sat under a tree to escape from the heat of the summer sun, and a line of ants ran over my knees and along the hem of my dress as we lay together on the grass. Michael lay on his back with his hands behind his head and asked me what I believed in.

I considered his question for a while, and then told him that I believed in stories.

He told me that he believed in Fate.

I said, 'Fate is for lazy people.'

He looked at me and shrugged.

When I was little, there was an old painting of the King of Bohemia hanging in the kitchen over a crack in the wall. It had been in the house when we first moved there, and next to it Vivien had hung a framed copy of the only letter that *The Times* ever chose to publish in her name, an observation of the lack of fire safety precautions which she had noted on her first visit to the Crystal Palace on Sydenham Hill in 1928.

In the painting, the King of Bohemia had thin hands and the largest calves I had ever seen. My dad told us that this king was unpopular with the Calvinists. He instructed us from the settee in the five doctrines of grace and dismissed predestination with a snort. He told us

31

that the King of Bohemia had commissioned two of his accomplices to govern Prague in his absence, and that these accomplices were put on trial by the Calvinists. I don't remember what the charges were, but the punishment consisted of immediate ejection from the castle window. The two men were found guilty and the sound of the bolt being drawn across the bottom of the window frame echoed through the courtroom.

This is the important bit. My dad would raise his head from the cushion and lower his voice and we would crouch closer to him as he told us that both men were reported as having survived the fall from the third-floor castle window. The king announced that the two men had been carried away by angels and deposited safely near Warsaw. The Calvinists believed no such thing. They claimed the men had landed in manure so soft that their lives were spared, and this was just another proof of sovereign grace. My dad had no patience with either the king or the Calvinists. He said that the men must have died. It was only rational. It was Newton.

I nodded and said nothing, but I thought he was wrong. In those days, I believed the king's story. It wasn't that I believed in miracles. I just believed in stories.

But now I have become practical. And I suppose that disappoints me a little.

My joints have turned to glass by the time Anna decides that it is time to leave. I extricate myself from the Business section with some difficulty and hobble next to her. I lose my nerve at the ticket barrier as I hear it crash behind

Anna and I refuse to go through, terrified, and embarrassed of my terror. I sneeze into the handkerchief that
I keep up my sleeve for such eventualities and she turns
and comes back to me.

We decide to get the bus home.

Michael

When we first met, I began by collecting an assortment of facts about her that I stored up and kept safe in a cardboard-box-shaped part of me. I wanted to know everything about her. I wanted to apply the techniques endorsed by the City & Guilds electrical courses that I pored over at night. I wanted to find ways of opening her up, observing her, passing electric currents through her and recording her reactions. It was the only way I knew.

I met her on a Wednesday in January. My father had left me in charge of the dairy, and I was sitting on the floor with my back against the wall and my legs stretched out under the counter, a heavy textbook balancing on my knee. I was reading about spectral lines, my neck aching with the effort of trying to memorise the frequencies at which streams of darkness could be detected in sunlight.

I was interrupted by a slightly impatient cough from behind the counter and I jumped as I hadn't heard anyone come in. I brushed myself down as I stood up, marking the page of my book by folding a table of frequencies into it. And then I looked at her for the first time.

She had bright blue eyes and a freckle under her eye that looked like a piece of dirt. Her eyelids were heavy and bold, and when she smiled her cheeks creased into deep dimples. She was dressed in overalls that were too big for her. The ends of her trousers trailed over and under her feet. The arms of her uniform were handless and wide. There was an embroidered slogan stitched half-heartedly onto her left breast pocket. She rolled up her sleeve and laid a small hand, dotted with freckles, on the counter. She smiled at me, and then she asked for two pints of milk.

I nodded stupidly. 'Do you live near here?'

'Quite near, but I don't normally come this way. I've just started working at the Sun Pat, you see.' She flapped her arm in the direction of the Old Kent Road and put the money on the counter. She gave me another dimply smile and pointed to the slogan on her oversized over-alls. 'See.'

'Peanuts,' I offered helpfully, thinking of the smell of roasting peanuts that lingered over Camberwell.

She nodded, smiling at me. 'Yes. Although actually I work in the canteen, chopping cabbages, because my mum thinks peanuts are dangerous.' She leaned conspir-atorially over the counter, her head tipped to one side so that the light reflected in her eyes, showing flecks of grey. 'She says it's no way to go, choking on a peanut.'

I grinned. 'She should try being trampled by a cow.' I bent down and removed my shoe and then lifted my socked foot onto the counter. 'See how flat it is? That's because a cow trod on it when I was five and my arches collapsed.'

She looked at me and raised an eyebrow. 'Both of them?'

I shrugged and nodded. 'Come and see the cows,' I

said, opening the back door of the shop and ushering her through. She stood next to me at the window, watching our four cows flicking their tails in the tiny field at the back of the shop, and she told me that her name was Stevie. I thought it was the most beautiful name I had ever heard.

When she left, I opened the door for her and thought of the obsequious bow that my father always performed for his customers. I leant out and called after her that we made chocolate milk on Thursdays. I saw her lift her hand to the side as she stepped off the pavement, as if in acknowledgement, but it may have been nothing at all. I picked up her coins from the counter and saw that she had given me slightly too much.

So that was how we met.

She came back a week later and I followed her around the shop, trying to elicit small pieces of information from her. A week later, she told me that she was scared of dogs and that her mother was allergic to cats. When my father was out, I showed her how to milk the cows and she jumped every time the milk squirted out into the bucket. She moved the stool round to the other side of the cow when she tried it, saying she couldn't do it from the same side as me because she was left-handed. She also told me that she bit her fingernails which infuriated her mother as it meant she could never be a nun. She held up her hand and laughed as she inspected her nails and I decided this must be a joke, although I remained ignorant as to the connection between her fingernails and her vocation.

My box of facts became gradually weightier and soon I could run my hands through my collection and feel them fall against each other as they slipped through my fingers. Occasionally I would tip all the pieces out and spread them across the floor, trying to fit them together. There were still a lot of gaps.

And finally, after seven weeks, I held my breath for three whole minutes while she smoothed her fingers over the packets of tea lined up next to the counter and then I asked her if she wanted to go to the pictures with me. She blushed and said yes, and I slotted that into my jigsaw.

Stevie

My mum discouraged love. Not as a general rule, just specifically in its romantic guise, its more obsessive form. She tutted at it, raised a solitary eyebrow at it, swept it to the back door and threw it down the step as if it were a crumb fallen from the mouth of a child.

She did grudgingly accept, in happy concord with the teachings of Saint Paul before her, that it was better to marry than to burn. But other than in the interests of preventing combustion, Vivien felt that the worst fate that could possibly befall a woman was to end up married with children.

She made my sister and I wear gloves on Sundays, even in the summer, scolding us that we would never get to be nuns if we wore bare hands to church, Anglican or not, and then we would have no way of seeing the world. We would be stuck in Peckham forever, she told us, unless we showed a willingness to convert.

'Nuns don't have fingernails like that,' she would proclaim, sending us back upstairs to find that our gloves were already laid out on the bed that we shared, waiting to be pulled daintily over the chewed ends of our fingers. 'And if they don't let you become a nun, there's no escape, no escape,' she would continue darkly, shaking her head as she dabbed the corner of the tea towel with her tongue and rubbed it roughly against the sticky corners of our mouths and the pencil smudges on our cheeks. It was a curious take on early feminism that Vivien had developed.

I tried it out at school, standing in front of the blackboard, my shirt tucked tightly into my skirt. The patent leather of my shoes shone brazenly against the wooden floorboards, evidence of a hard-won victory in the shoe shop, a victory qualified by promises to scuff the leather and never shine them so that the colour of my underwear would not be displayed in the reflections on my toes as I walked about town.

'When I grow up, I'd like to be a nun.'

I could feel my cheeks flushing. Joanna Overton, who had just announced to the whole class that when she grew up she wanted to be a jug of water, rudely fell off her chair at the back of the room through laughing so much. I thought that was a bit rich. I grinned to show that I didn't mind, baring my teeth perhaps a little over-zealously. And I really didn't mind. I was just testing it, seeing how it tasted when I said it out loud. I didn't mention it at school again.

But in spite of my concerned teacher reporting my religious ambition to Vivien, I showed an early propensity for love that bothered my mum deeply. I became fixated with the coalman when I was seven, an occasional, overpowering sensation that came in torrents and disappeared as soon as it had come. I would be going about my normal business, cutting pirates' hats for my brothers out of newspaper or writing stories diagonally across pieces of paper, when I would hear the coalshed door being dragged across the concrete of the yard. I would be out like a shot. There was no amount of pre-emptive barricades that Vivien could construct to keep me away from the coalman, no amount of interest shown in my creations that could distract me from my course.

He never spoke to anyone. He simply tipped the peak of his cap as the questions followed him to the coalsheds. 'How are you?' 'Cup of tea?' 'Cold, isn't it?' All were answered simply by a tip, and this slow gesture was applied in relation to all weather systems. Only once did he take the cup of tea that Vivien offered, leaving a trail of black dust in the shadow where his arm had been extended to the kitchen door to take the proffered mug. His mug went on a separate shelf after that, in case he ever wanted another one.

It was his face that I loved. A portrait of a face, its lines defined in charcoal and the rest shaded in with grey pencil, a face that had been dropped onto a hard floor and meticulously glued back together. I would wait for him out in the street, next to his horse, hopping from foot to foot on the pavement.

He stopped coming when I was eight. There was a new coalman – a short, chubby man who perspired easily, streaking the dust across his face so that it looked like the night sky with a storm brewing. The new man talked as he filled the coalshed, talked as he tipped his cap, talked as he climbed onto his cart, and undoubtedly continued to talk as the cart rolled away down the road. I was not impressed. Vivien was relieved to see how quickly I became immune to the sound of the coalshed door scraping on the yard as it opened. She thought I was fickle and it delighted her.

I had forgotten about the coalman until I met Michael. The first time we went to the pictures he walked home with me afterwards, my hand curled up in his. And as he turned to walk away I found myself going with him, dragged along like a cart attached to a horse as far as the end of the road, before reluctantly unpicking my fingers and running back home. I hadn't told Vivien about him. I didn't want her to worry. I pretended I was going to the cinema with a thick-necked girl I had known at primary school of whom she approved for reasons I had never been able to grasp.

But Vivien must have suspected something. She didn't ever ask me directly about Michael but she started following me around the house. She watched me sipping my tea, her eyes wide and her mouth slightly open, as if there was something she wanted to say. She borrowed a French grammar from the library and suggested that I learn French if I was bored at the factory. Of course, I was bored and yet at the same time I wasn't because I filled my days with thoughts of Michael, of the way he pulled at the collar of my coat before kissing me, of the feeling in my stomach when he touched my neck, his fingers soft and cold. It swelled inside me like an illness, a bloated liver or an enlarged kidney.

And when eventually he didn't come back, Vivien nodded knowingly and said nothing.

It was different with Jonathan. When he first came to visit, Vivien lined cups of tea along the arm of his chair and presented him with a peeled clementine and a saucer of raisins, both of which had been bitterly fought for at the grocer's that morning. She flattened her hair with licked fingertips and narrowed her eyes at me when I mentioned Emily. Her eyes shone with desperation as she waved him goodbye at the door. She had already decided that, nunnery being off the cards, he would have to do.

Michael

Anna has replaced Doreen today. She turns on the light
when she comes in to wake me up, cushioning the switch
with her fingers so that it is almost silent. At visiting
time I ask her if she will turn me round so that I can
look out of the window. I write my request on the pad
that hangs from a string next to my bed. I tell her I feel
like a gooseberry. She puts her hands on her hips and
says I am being ridiculous. She says the bed is too heavy,
and that anyway it isn't ward policy to have people
looking out of the window. Doreen insists that everyone
must face inwards.

I tell her I thought it was a cancer ward, not a psychi-
atric one. She blows out amusedly through her nose but
still refuses to turn me. I would turn myself, but it's
difficult.

So I lie here with my eyes shut, feigning noncha-
lance, my glasses resting on the bump of my nose so
that my surreptitious glances are in focus. I flap my
ears with my fingers so as to hear a little better the
sanitised news of Neighbourhood Watch meetings and
primary school plays, straining my neck to see the gifts
they bring, small helium balloons that are left to shrivel
on bedposts and magazines that cater for the barely

literate. I devour these magazines once they have been dipped in tea and stickily discarded by their original owners, and they shock and bore me all at once, leaving splashes of colour across my eyes that refuse to be rubbed away.

'Where are your family?' Anna asks me, as she lines up my medicines on the table. 'Do you want me to tell someone that you're here?'

I haven't decided how much I am going to tell her yet. *They've all gone*, I write.

'I'm so sorry.'

Don't be. It's my own fault. I don't mean to be melo-dramatic. It just comes out a little like that when I put it in writing.

'Did you kill them?'

I can't tell if she is joking. She doesn't seem to be but that is not the sort of question healthcare assistants should ask. Perhaps she is autistic. I have read an article about that in one of those magazines.

I shake my head.

She laughs. 'Well, it's not your fault then, is it?' She walks away without looking back, and leaves me flat-tened against my headboard.

Is it not?

She comes back twirling a stolen flower between her finger and thumb. A round-faced, purple-headed flower with a leafless stalk, purloined from an oversized bouquet stuffed with backcombed grasses and open-mouthed lilies. She says that the flower is too postmodern for such gaudy accompaniments.

I like my flower. It stands placidly in a thin vase next to my bed and watches over me. I count its petals. She

44

loves me not. She loves me. I put a small pen mark at my starting point so that I know where to finish, and I flick the petals as I incant.

She loves me not.

Anna is talking to me again. The drugs distract me and make me sleepy. She smells of mottled rubber and her name badge is upside down.

ɐuu∀

She is pretty, my Anna. Yesterday I woke to find her standing next to the window and I thought I was dreaming, but when she turned I saw that she had only one dimple and I remembered. She has light brown freckles on her face and hands and dark brown hair that she ties back at the top of her head, slightly off-centre. I don't know if that is deliberate. But it looks nice.

I write, *She loves me not* on a piece of paper and hand it to her, gesturing towards the flower. She looks at me and laughs. 'Then you should start with the one you didn't start with last time.'

You see, she is clever too, my Anna.

I have developed a strange reputation in the ward. Enigmatic through my enforced silence. The nurses have decorated the space around my bed with cardboard signs, listing a series of 'episodes'. Michael does not talk. Michael does not like to be rushed. Michael does not like broccoli. Michael dislikes abrupt movements. Michael does not like the light being switched on and off. Relevant and defining traits for communal, hospital living. People tiptoe around me as if my silence is nothing more than an aversion to noise. Do they really think that people stay silent because they don't like noise?

But Anna is different from the other nurses, just as I had known she would be. She teases me, and ruffles my head as if it still has a few curls at the edges. Which it doesn't. There is more hair growing out of my ears than out of my head.

She sits on my bed and takes my flower from its vase. She begins to chant in a soft whisper. He loves me. He loves me not. She completes the circle and grins at me. He loves me. She puts it back. And then leaves me.

She is right. I do love her and it makes me want to be more than I am. But I have a sneaking suspicion that there is not enough time. I shut my eyes and pretend to sleep.

Stevie

The problem was that my mum married the wrong Reg. My dad arrived on her doorstep one Sunday afternoon in 1919, scraping his feet on the step and whistling nervously as she looked at him through the letterbox before she opened the door. He had shiny hair and windswept shoes and a demob suit of navy blue that lay heavily across his shoulders. He sat silently in the front room and flapped his hand across his mug of tea to cool it before gulping it loudly. My dad told her that he was a friend of her brother Jack, and that they had fought together in the Great War. He mentioned that his aunt lived in the next road along and so, while he was there, he had decided to call, to pay his respects.

Of course, Vivien Taylor was not my mum yet. She was just a girl dressed in a cream cardigan that buttoned all the way up to her neck, but which she left half open because when it was done all the way up it made her look like a poodle. She had a half-day every Sunday, and on those days she came home to cook for her family instead of cooking for the Willesden-Walkers in Chelsea. She liked cooking at home because she could wear her cardigan instead of a stiff apron and a cap that covered her ears and muffled the voices of the other maids in the kitchen.

Vivien had heard about a Reg from Jack's letters. He emerged from her brother's wobbly writing, pressed into straight lines on thin paper, dotted with holes where the tip of the pen had fallen through onto his spindly knee as he wrote. She read of a Reg who drew pictures of horses in fields of flowers, and who made whistles from long pieces of grass that he found at the edges of roads, and who read aloud to her brother at night when he couldn't sleep. Jack told her that she would like Reg.

But Jack hadn't made it. And Vivien had become a maid in a big house with a shed in the garden. She went with Reg to Brockwell Park, to the lake where she and Jack had played as children. Vivien talked about her brother and Reg listened. They left footprints in the frost and the cold air seeped in through the ends of their noses and into their faces, turning them redder than blushes. Vivien was disappointed that he didn't pick any of the long grasses that swayed next to the geese by the lake to make into whistles. They stopped talking for a while and the sky turned pink. Vivien thought that perhaps he was shy, or had left all his stories in a field in Northern France.

Their footprints had melted into squashed green blades by the time they turned back. On the way home Reg told her that he had just got a job as a driver for the London Underground and that he was happy because being underground made him feel safer. He told Vivien that he was going to be put on the Metropolitan Railway Line that ran across the top of the city, through Baker Street and St Pancras.

I don't think that Vivien Taylor would have consented to walk the paths of the Royal Parks the following Sunday had Reg not then proceeded to inform her that St Pancras was a young Roman who had been beheaded in AD 304 for being a Christian, and had since become the patron saint of headaches. She started to laugh, which made Reg fidgety and talkative. He told her that the bodily trunk of the young St Pancras had been mislaid but his head was still on display in a basilica in Rome, should she care to pay it a visit. She imagined a twirling parasol and a lilac ribbon in her hair and hot feet on marble stones.

He took her arm nervously and told her of another unfortunate beheaded saint who also patronised headaches, Anastasias the Persian (né Magundat), who had first been strangulated in preparation for the disembodiment. It was the way he said 'né' that enraptured Vivien Taylor. She began to hiccup. By the time they arrived home, she had hot palms and could no longer feel the bunion on her left foot.

She invited him for tea the next Sunday and spent the afternoon queuing at the butcher's with a blue bowl under her arm. She asked for extra sausages to go in the toad-in-the-hole she was planning to make. She hummed as she sifted the lumps out of the flour. It felt a little bit like having Jack back home. Reg arrived at six o'clock with red cheeks and fluffy hair, and Vivien smelt the steam from the Peckham baths on his neck. That was his effort.

My dad later said that he married my mum because of her cooking. Vivien knew how to transform turnips into syrupy chunks that tasted of exotic and spiky fruits, and how to make hot soups thick with boiled onion skins, and she knew that lentils could pass for mince-meat if you covered them with mashed potato and grilled them to the right shade of brown. She would smile glassily when my dad said this and he would put his arm round her, pulling her into his chest, as if he was only joking.

And Vivien agreed to marry him because she thought he was a different Reg. She told me that just after he died. I blame Uncle Jack for not being sufficiently clear in his letters. He should have used full names and given descriptions of physical attributes. But he didn't. He wasn't to know, after all.

My mum married the wrong Reg on a yellow Saturday in May. She met the real Reg over trifle in the church hall after the ceremony, when it was too late. She had made the trifles herself. The old lady who lived next door to Auntie Vera had offered to make them but had died the week before, and no one had thought it proper to address the subject of trifles to the executor of her affairs. But Vivien Taylor had always imagined there would be small trifles in little glass bowls at her wedding so she made them herself that morning, her apron tied around the pink dress that she would be wearing to the church.

The chairs were stacked at the side of the hall and an array of cousins and family acquaintances were sitting on tables with their legs swinging. There were a few people dancing self-consciously in front of the gramophone. A young man she had never met before came over to the trifle table and held out his hand to her. 'You must be Viv.' He had red cheeks and Irish eyelashes.

She nodded, and held his hand for a little bit longer than was altogether proper for a newly wedded woman. He told her that he had been in the war with Her Reg, as people had already started referring to her husband, and had fought in the division that her husband had played the pipes for. It came as a surprise to Vivien Ponder (née Taylor) that her new husband had not actually fought in the war, but had been the official piper who piped the boys over the top and watched them being brought back. It struck Vivien as a remarkable thing that they would take a piper. Did it not spoil the element of surprise somewhat? She realised that her husband had never spoken about the war during their engagement.

She said that she was pleased to meet any of her husband's friends and handed him a dove-tailed serviette to go with his trifle. The young man took it, letting the tail flatten out as he told her that he had come to see her, not the groom. He handed her an envelope with her name written on it, scrawled dramatically in slanting letters. He dug his spoon into his trifle and scooped the jelly from the bottom of the trifle bowl, trying to avoid surplus cream. And underneath her name it said '(For Jack's sister)'. She looked at him in surprise, and he told her that Jack had been his best friend and he had started the letter to her in a hospital in Blackburn a year ago and had spent so long thinking about what to write that he had only managed to finish it whilst sitting on a bench at Euston station that morning. He apologised for not having sent it sooner.

'Thank you . . .' she hesitated. 'I'm sorry, I don't know your name.'

'Reginald,' he said, 'But everyone calls me Reg. The same as your husband.'

Another Reg. Jack had known two of them. She felt her stomach fall, and she looked at her new husband standing with his back slumped and his feet turned slightly outwards, one of them tapping against the wooden floor, spooning cream into his mouth.

The real Reg put down his bowl. He turned to leave, but then stopped and leant over the trifles to whisper in her ear. 'I'm sorry, I can't stay. I have to get back. I just wanted to meet you.' He hesitated and then quickly grabbed her hand and brushed his lips across it, almost kissing her, and then he said quietly, 'Jack never mentioned his sister was so beautiful. The piper is a lucky man.'

Vivien Ponder smiled as he dropped her hand and walked away, leaving her upturned face the colour of her rose-pink wedding dress. She walked slowly to the ladies' lavatory in the church hall and waited for the women at the mirror to leave the room before turning the key in the lock and letting a small tear push its way out from the corner of one eye. She wiped it carefully with the edge of a finger. She folded the letter into her bag and combed her hair, sliding a brown hairgrip above her left ear to keep the hair from falling onto her cheek. She put her arms around her waist.

'Oh Jack. You silly ass. Why didn't you tell me there were two of them? Please tell me that you liked the piper a little bit as well.'

There was a knock on the door. She breathed out slowly and tilted her head in front of the mirror, examining her eyes to check for traces of red. She opened the door and went back to join her husband and the dancing, her smile shining only a little dimmer on her lips than it had done before the trifle had been served.

There was not a day that went by during which Vivien did not wonder what her life would have been like with the other Reg. She looked at my dad, lying on the couch in the middle of the day as she added nips to the waists of ladies' skirts, and she wondered. She closed her ears to the sound of him practising his pipes, and turned sideways whenever he came too close.

From that day onwards, Vivien's guard was raised. She was adamant that this would not happen to her girls.

Michael

'Go on then. You do it yourself. I'm not looking.'

The soap slips between my nervous fingers as I take it from her and I drop it in the bath. I feel small and childish. Her hands are on her hips and her elbows intimidate me. The air hangs like a low cloud between us. The soap slithers down to my feet and I feel it brushing against my toes.

Anna reaches in and pulls the soap out. 'I've seen it all before, you know.' She hands it to me again and then turns around.

There is something about the idea of full submersion that I find alluring. The noise of one's bottom sliding down, bumping along the surface of the tub. Loose hairs floating outwards, clinging to the surface of the water like algae. And the silence. I like that sort of silence. Clean and deliberate. It's a different sort of silence from the one that bounces around a nearly empty room when the radio is on, muffled only slightly by the illusion of company provided by Radio 4. *The Afternoon Play*. *The Archers*. *Gardeners' Question Time*. That's a different sort of silence altogether.

But, according to Doreen, one is not allowed to completely submerge oneself in the hospital. It is against the regulations. And it is physically impossible, thus making the regulations easier to follow. The bath is too cramped. My legs are concertinaed against the officious-looking taps. I would need another set of knees if I were going to lie completely flat against the floor of the bath.

Anna is wiping my back with a huge sponge that smells of the North Sea.

'They organised the French Revolution from the bath. Or at least, one of them organised a bit of it from the bath, the bit after the revolution. This man,' she paused, 'whose name I can't remember, used to lie in the bath writing death lists of people to go to the guillotine. Until someone, a girl, came in and stabbed him with a knife. And that was that. There's a painting of that bit.'

She delves into my ears with soapy fingers and dabs the hairs on the back of my head with a drop of shampoo.

'Of course, he was ill. That's why he always stayed in the bath. He had a disease which he caught in a sewer that made his skin flake like the pastry of a sausage roll. So it was better when he was in the bath.'

She takes the shower and sprays the top of my head. The water seeps into my eyes and feels sticky against my skin. I breathe it in by mistake and begin to cough.

'And it's funny because there was that French singer who died in the bath as well, with a hairdryer or a toaster or something. Which is odd, as I didn't think French people liked toast.'

She pulls out the plug and the water begins to drain away. I hold onto the handles at the side of the bath to stop myself from swirling. The thought of a watery death is making me feel confined and shaky.

'She bought the knife from a shop over the road. And

she was guillotined later for having murdered him.' She stops and looks at me for a moment. 'I'm sorry. Do you want to get out?'

I nod my head.

'I didn't mean to upset you. I just thought it was a good story. We've been learning about it at college. The French Revolution, I mean, not the man with the toaster.'

I nod again, to reassure her. It is a good story, I want to tell her. I can't control my shaking. And it's not the story. It's not the image of the swirl of blood in the bath-water that is making me shake. Or the toaster. At least, it's not either of those things specifically. It's just that there are new ways of dying I hadn't thought of before, and now I will have to think of them when I am trying to sleep. I will have to add them to my list.

I am panicking again. White clouds. White clouds. White clouds. I repeat it over and over again in my head, hoping that the repetition will drive everything else out, and leave the backs of my eyes white and edgeless. I feel hands gripping my ankles, arms thrown around my chest, and a stab in my shoulder. Then nothing at all.

I wake up in my bed, dreaming of wet sheep. My left arm aches. Anna is sitting on a chair. She is wearing a thick woollen jumper over her uniform and is scribbling on a pad of paper. She jumps when I move my hand.

'I'm so sorry,' she says. 'I don't know why I was wittering on like that.'

I flap my hand at her. It's okay, I want to say. Let's not talk about it. I can hardly lift my arm.

'Your arm might be a bit numb after the injection. They had to do it, but it was just a small sedative.' She seems nervous. She stuffs her notebook into her bag. I point at it, trying to change the subject.

'This?' she asks. 'It's a history essay. It's due in tomorrow.'

I frown at her.

'I'm not a nurse, you know. Just a healthcare assistant. I'm still at college. This is just sort of work experience because I want to be a doctor. You need to put it on your form.'

I tap excitedly on the side of my bed. I had not guessed that she wanted to be a doctor. I am bursting with pride.

She misunderstands my taps and hands me the piece of paper she has been scribbling on. 'It's about the French Revolution. The man I was telling you about in the bath.' She hesitates and looks at me. 'His name was Marat. I looked it up. But the bit about the bath isn't in there. My teacher says it's not important.'

I roll my eyes at her and she laughs. Her writing is scruffy and cynical. It is too small to read. I hand it back to her and she lifts herself from the chair. 'I have to go now. I just wanted to see that you were, you know, okay.' I nod and try to smile, frustrated by my silence.

When she leaves, I take the pad that is hanging next to my pillow and balance it on my stomach and I begin to write in shaky capitals that wobble off the edges of the pages and imprint themselves on the pages underneath.

Dear Anna. There is something you should know.

I hesitate and cross it out. The notepaper smells of smeared carrots. In fact, now that I think of it, the whole hospital is drenched in the smell of mashed and watery carrots. I hide my nose in my blanket but the smell seeps in pervasively through the stitching. It is the first thing I notice when I wake up in the mornings. Sometimes I only know for certain that I am still alive because I can still smell them.

I try again. I try to write more lightly but I drop my pencil and incite a glassy smile from Doreen when I push the emergency button to draw her attention to it.

Dear Anna. There is something I need to tell you.

I pause. I watch the rest of them in the ward, rustling softly as they prepare themselves for sleep. I watch them folding their hands and shutting their eyes. I see their lips twitching with half-spoken prayers and still I watch them, wondering at their complacency. How can they be so calm? Have none of them heard the list my father taught me when I was six years old?

The lights go out and I can no longer see. I tear off the piece of paper and screw it up, letting the notepad fall so that it swings next to me on its string. Tomorrow. I will start tomorrow.

I sleep facing inwards, as instructed, dreaming of all the things I would write to her if I only knew where to begin.

Stevie

I have always had a thing about toothbrushes. I can't bear splayed bristles clogged with dried toothpaste. It makes me nauseous to hear the hawkings and swillings of others, to watch the white froth gathering and bubbling over their tongues. My toothbrush is immaculate. I wipe the stalk of it with a flannel after every session, and flick the bristles with my finger until the spray is clear again, and then I put it back in its shiny glass next to the sink.

It is a small thing, this obsession. I did not even know it was there until Jonathan and I moved in together after we were married and he started using my toothbrush interchangeably with his, leaving its bristles encrusted with off-white paste. I tried hiding it, camouflaging it among the leaves of the spider plant on the windowsill or in the flowery jug above the bath, but still he would seek it out and use it. I would find it lying in a small puddle of diluted toothpaste in the soap dish next to the sink and it would leave me dizzy with rage.

Jonathan's toothbrush is still lying on the side of the bath where he left it. I pick it up between my finger and thumb and hold it above the bin, but I cannot let go. Instead I lift it to my nose, searching for the smell of him, a clue to give me somewhere to begin, a way of remembering what he looked like. I mean, what he *really* looked like. I have got photographs, but they're not the same, are they?

I don't know how I can have forgotten so soon. When I think of my husband, the first thing that comes to me are the two diagonal scars he had on either side of his neck, remnants of the secondary tuberculosis he had as a child. The surgeon had to remove two golf-ball sized lumps from his throat. Those were the days when milk was drunk straight from the udder. I can picture the whorls of black hair that grew fuzzily and comfortingly out of his body at every opportunity. And the scar on his leg, where the shrapnel got him, and the jagged lines of it across his foot. I can see the hairs on the tops of his toes and the sides of his hands. I have lined his clothes up limply along the front of the wardrobe, baggy brown corduroy trousers and flat red shirts. Scuffed shoes standing at ten to two.

So I can remember some things. It is just his face I have lost. I shall open my window for a little while and watch for bats.

My memory started to disappear when Jonathan became ill. I sanded my memories down, removing the rough edges that might cut if they were held too tightly or brushed carelessly against. I began to forget things on purpose. Jonathan was never very good at factual recall. It was always up to me to remember birthdays and road layouts. His memories were shadowy shapes, washed smooth like pebbles. We began telling each other the same stories, over and over again, so there were no surprises.

But I remember the day we went to get the results of

60

his tests. I remember standing up too quickly. I remember white neon filling the space behind my eyes. Hospital lights. Bright walls. Pale faces and a scrubbed coat. My husband standing straight-backed and open-mouthed as the doctor bent over me, coaxing my eyes open, whispering to me that I had to be strong. Strong? I thought of dumb-bells lifted above heads and bearskins and oily chests. I blinked and wondered where I would start.

From that moment on we talked only of the practicalities of illness. Bowel movements and hot heads. The trappings of a fast slow death. Appetite. Which pyjamas he wanted for his birthday. We didn't speak about what was coming next. We each held it close like a secret we did not want the other to find out, arranging our words neatly around it so that they did not bump or touch, until one day the secret crashed into us when we had forgotten to look out for it and I was left all alone.

He didn't ever lose his eyesight entirely. He could still see colours and light and the look on my face, but words on pages became difficult for him. I read out loud to him every day. We started with bendy Wordsworth Classics whose breathless sentences sent us both to sleep, and we moved on to the American Beat poets after the young man at the library recommended them. Once I had got used to reading their casual blasphemies out loud, I began to find them surprisingly liberating. I started muttering under my breath in an American accent. I announced to Emily the other day that I thought the Avon lady was a real sonovabitch.

Jonathan liked Jack Kerouac best. I went to the shop and bought a packet of Lucky Strikes for him to smoke while I read, and he emptied them out of their cellophane packet onto the bed, smoothing the paper of the fatly luxurious cigarettes with his fingers. He hadn't smoked for years, not since I had removed the limp and crispy roll-up that hung from his lips on the day Emily and I moved into his house in Orpington and told him that there were some things I would not tolerate in front of my daughter. He had simply nodded and kissed me, and told me that I only had to ask.

After a while, I started smoking Lucky Strikes too, just to join in. I let my cigarette burn in the ashtray that we balanced on the duvet between us and took shallow asthmatic gulps, trying to swallow the smoke and hold it in until enough time had passed and I could let it out again. He taught me how to inhale, how to breathe the smoke fully into my pulmonary arteries, and how to blow smoke rings that shimmered and rose like gentle snores. We lay on the bed together between chapters and held hands. We shut our eyes and let our breath fall in clouds around us as our necks turned blue and veiny.

It was Emily who found the mail order tapes of talking magazines and ordered a curious selection for us to listen to. We spent whole days lying in our smoky bed, shutting our eyes and sniggering ungenerously at the pedantry of the *History Today* reader. We grew accustomed to falling asleep to the dulcet tones of the *National Geographic*, dreaming of gestating camels and the moist eyes of stick-insects.

I hardly even noticed that Jonathan was becoming thinner every day, gradually flattening against the bed like an unsmoked roll-up trodden underfoot.

*

I haven't cancelled the order to the talking magazines since he died. I find them comforting now that he is no longer here. When he was ill, I didn't think about how I was going to cope without him. It was Jonathan I worried about. I thought I would be fine. I was ready for loneliness and sadness and all the other things you expect.

But, now that it has happened, it is the silence that surprises me most. It startles me with its echoes, making me jump when I am not ready for them. I have developed ways of coping. I leave the radio on all night. I talk to myself in the mirror. I continue to read books out loud, doing voices and emphasising all the adverbs. But still my mouth is heavy. It is filled with strange lumps that I cannot swallow.

I lay Jonathan's toothbrush back in the soap dish and phone the doctor's surgery to make an appointment. Emily has been telling me to do this for weeks.

I go the next day. The GP is new, a young man with a pale face and wispy hair who nods in all the wrong places and then hands me a prescription, two a day to be taken with a milky drink. I stare at him and he grins nervously, wanting me to leave. As I reach the door, he spins suddenly in his chair and suggests that I try a new hobby.

'I'm not a French exchange student,' I mutter crossly.

'But what do you like doing, Mrs Sandford?' His voice is reedy and over-educated.

'Reading.'

'Anything more sociable? Bowls perhaps?'

I sigh and pretend that I will join the local bowling

club. As I leave I wonder whether, if I were to take all my new tablets at the same time, it would be enough.

But I know I won't really do that. I'm not the sort. I don't like abruptness.

I don't like endings either.

Michael

It is lunchtime. Anna is pushing the food trolley through the ward and distributing small bowls and plastic spoons. She flourishes a gaudy yellow bowl from her trolley and hands it to me. 'Egg,' she says. 'Again.'

I watch her go and then look hopefully into my bowl. The egg is porridgey and beige. The yellow has seeped out of it and into the bowls that are lined up jauntily on Anna's trolley. We have had egg every day this week. I would prefer toast, but nobody ever comes to take my order. Or fried eggs with blackened edges and small bubbles in the white bits, like we used to cook on the scorching bonnets of our army trucks in Africa. I remember how they smelt, of linoleum and aprons and scoured frying pans, and how the smell made us look at each other in surprise, suddenly uncertain how we had ended up in the highlands of North Africa in desert shorts and heavy boots with nervous twitches in our necks.

I balance the bowl on my stomach and scrabble in the shoebox I keep next to my bed. I have kept everything. Linen-backed telecommunications maps of Africa, photographs and bus tickets, ledgers detailing training schedules for my pigeons in Lewisham, and a pile of old letters from Stevie. I see her words lying faintly where she pressed them, bleached by time into parched shadows on the paper, echoing like familiar songs as I glance at them. I snap the elastic band around the bundle and tuck it back into the side of the box.

I leaf through my small hoard of photographs until I find the one I am looking for. It was taken during our push northwards in 1941, just outside Mogadishu. People did not smile for pictures in those days. That is a relatively new phenomenon. Instead we are squinting severely at the camera, balancing our metallic-tasting eggs between wedges of sun-hardened bread. The bonnet of the truck behind us is streaked with lard. I have my right arm draped over Brendan's shoulder, and he is leaning into me. His cap is pulled forward in a self-conscious attempt to cover his hair, but still it creeps out over his ears.

I push the emergency button next to my headboard to call Anna back in.

She shuts the curtain behind her conspiratorially and I give her the photograph. She balances it delicately between her fingers and runs her eyes along the row of faces. 'Is that you?'

I nod.

'You look so young. And you have hair and teeth. Quite a looker.'

I smile and shrug in what I imagine to be a modest manner.

'Where were you when this was taken?'

I write on my pad. *Africa*.

'During the war?'

I nod again.

'I always forget that the war was in Africa as well.' She looks a little sheepishly at me. 'I'm sorry. I suppose you wouldn't really forget, would you?'

I show her another one, a later one, in which I am standing next to a pigeon loft in Cairo. She takes it and squints at it, her nose creasing endearingly.

'You looked after pigeons in the war?'

Only after, I write.

'After what?' she asks.

I hesitate. My pen hovers above the page. I have not yet decided how much I want her to know. I write his name. *Alf*.

She looks at me blankly. 'Who's Alf? A friend?'

I go back to the first photograph and point to the man on my left. My other arm is resting on him and he is looking behind my head, distracted by something outside the edges of the picture. His hair is plastered to his head with sweat and he is laughing, bending slightly and leaning on my shoulder. She lifts the photograph to her face and runs her fingers along the row of faces.

'You all look so young,' she says again.

There is a shout and a crash from outside the cubicle. Anna looks up guiltily. 'Oh, I have to go. I was supposed to be holding something while the doctor inserted a catheter.' She stops at the curtain and throws me an apologetic glance as she leaves. I sigh and lie back and moisten my gums with egg.

Stevie

It is two weeks since Jonathan's funeral and my daughter is waiting for me in the library foyer. She has that purposeful glint in her eye that I saw the very first time she opened her eyes and looked at me. It was there every day, shining determinedly, until the day Scott told her he was leaving because he had met someone else. It was as if he had leant towards her and pinched that glint between the pointed ends of his finger and thumb and plucked it out of her.

I see the glint even before I notice the empty suitcase she is wheeling primly behind her as she walks over to me, and I smile because it has been months since I have seen her eyes shining like that.

'Where are we going?'

'You're coming to live with me.'

'Can't I stay at home?' I say it out of habit, so that when I relent and grudgingly allow Emily to take me to her house she will feel that she has won some sort of victory. This has been a contentious topic ever since Jonathan died. My obstinacy infuriates her. She thinks that I have wallowed for long enough. Wallowing is only of use to the wallower if it is agreed upon as a temporary measure, according to my daughter.

I don't tell her that I had already decided to relent the next time she asked. We go back to my house and I watch the bus stop from the car window as Emily sets timers on the lamps and collects stockings and cardigans from my drawers. She is small and practical, my daughter, with soft muscles in her freckly arms and her hair is richly brown. She has, I notice, coloured in the grey bits again.

That man has not been at the bus stop for nearly two weeks now. I wonder what has happened to him.

We get fish and chips to celebrate my arrival at Emily's which we eat from the wrapper at the kitchen table. Our fingers are shiny from the grease of the chips and they slip against each other. Emily looks up triumphantly as I make appreciative noises whilst ladling spoonfuls of tasteless cod into my mouth. She looks at me with the expression of someone who has just caught a large trout. I think she is pleased to have me.

'Where's Anna?' I ask, standing up to get a mug from the cupboard above the sink.

'Out.' Emily frowns and stabs a chip. 'Visiting Scott. She sees him on Tuesdays after college.'

'Oh,' I say, my fingers brushing the bottom of the shelf as I stretch up, trying to reach. 'I thought she didn't want to see him.'

'She says it's easier, that it's less hassle just to agree to see him once a week than have him phoning all the time. And she thinks he might listen to her. She thinks she can persuade him not to sell the house.' She shrugs and puts the chip in her mouth. 'But she can't.'

I snort in sceptical agreement and give up on my attempt to retrieve the glass, unable to get any purchase. 'You never know,' I offer unconvincingly.

Emily shakes her head and stands up abruptly. 'Come on, I'll get that down for you.' She stands up and hands the mug down to me. 'You're getting smaller, Mum.'

'I know.'

I have been shrinking for a while now. My ends are pressed in on themselves, like a smoked stub. At home I have to line the cups up in rows at the front of the cupboards because I can no longer reach the backs of them and I keep a chair next to the cooker to reach the plates.

Emily installs me in the spare room along with a pile of peach-coloured tissues. The bed is in the middle of the room, pointing towards the window. There are flowers printed on the sheets and embroidered on the cushions that encircle my head. There are flowers pressed inside the dictionary next to the bed, just as Vivien taught Emily to do when she was a child. There are daffodils on the windowsill and crocuses in the fireplace. I feel as if I am lying in a meadow. Emily brings me a teacup of warm milk with flowers painted on the handle, and I sneeze myself to sleep.

In the morning I wake up and, for a booming, flowery second, I forget where I am. I could be anywhere in the world. I reach my hand over to the pillow next to mine, eager to find out, but when I grasp for Jonathan's shoulder I find there is nothing there and instead my hand flops onto a thorny stem printed on the duvet cover. I look up and see the empty teacup next to my bed, and then I remember.

Michael

I owe a lot of things to Brendan Hardcastle.

If you were to pass no more than a cursory glance in his direction, you might consider him to be something of an unlikely hero. You might see a small boy wearing wiry spectacles too high on his nose, and socks pulled tightly up to his knees. His hair was coarse and springy and was a startling shade of red that I have never seen on any other head than his. He always wore a tie, even on Saturdays, and he had a curious habit of rocking from foot to foot when he stood up.

But Brendan Hardcastle could balance a football on the back of his neck and do backwards somersaults from standing. He knew how engines worked. He had a beautiful sister and no dad. When he spoke, people listened, and it embarrassed him.

When I first joined St Francis's School, I followed my brother Ben around and played football with his friends in the playground. They were old enough to only pretend to tackle me as I charged towards them, spindly-legged and flat-footed and too long in the toe, and Ben would grin at me and ruffle the back of my head when nobody was watching.

When Ben died, I no longer felt like playing football.

My mother told me that I should try to make some friends, but Ben was my yardstick and nobody else quite matched up. Every day Brendan Hardcastle came over to where I was sitting on the low brick wall that ran around the playground, and asked me to play. And every day I refused politely and lowered my small nose back into whichever inappropriate volume I had borrowed from the school library. I attempted to read until the bell rang and then I would line up at the back of the queue and file back to the classroom.

I could not explain to anyone that I missed Ben with a force I could not name. It felt like I was being poked in the side with a large stick. It put me off my food and deadened the muscles in my cheeks.

Brendan lived two doors down from me. He would run ahead with the other boys while I walked behind, but then he would wait for me at the corner of our road, standing on his hands and balancing his heels against the wall of the house on the corner. His face was streaky and blotchy in places from running.

He would follow me down the entry into our yard and we would kick a football against the back wall, taking turns to hit it into pebbly corners and then scrambling after it. There were rusting bike wheels and small flowers in cracked terracotta pots in the middle of the yard that we would rearrange to make the game more interesting. I would diligently try to use the inside of my foot in the way he instructed me to, but my connections were unreliable and there were never very many heads on the flowers in the pots. My legs would grow tired before his, and I would climb to the top of the wall which separated the yard from the field where we kept the cows, and I would sit with my back against the top of the door-frame to watch him.

Brendan would leave when we heard my father closing the dairy, and bolting the front door loudly. He would walk along the wall that joined the backs of our houses together, his arms outstretched like a comedian in a crackly film reel. When he was standing above his own yard, he would get to his knees and hang from his fingers, grinning at me as I climbed meticulously down via the toilet shed roof.

When I was about twelve, it occurred to me that I had never been inside Brendan's house. His front door was made from bumpy glass in a maroon frame and was rarely opened. People moved like ghosts behind it.

One day, Brendan's front door was open and Brendan was standing on a crate reaching up to the sheltered bit of wall under the gutter, his tie gripping his neck and pulling against him. He had sticky tape plastered in strips to his chin and to the sides of his glasses and he was grimacing in an attempt to keep all the bits of sticky tape away from each other. He was holding a cardboard box with a red circle and a green circle cut into it and wires stretching messily into the house. His hair stood out brightly against the door.

I sat on the matching maroon gate and watched him, running my legs along the floor and then kicking them out so that the gate swung on its hinges until it jolted to a halt. He stepped down and pushed his glasses up to the bridge of his nose.

'What's it for?' I asked.

He looked at me and at the flowerpot that I had

knocked over with my swinging feet and then down the street.

'It's a door entry system that I've invented. It's a birthday present for my mum.'

'Why?'

He shrugged and adjusted his spectacles. 'So that people know when to leave her alone. She doesn't always like having visitors, old people and milkmen and people like that. She isn't always . . .' He paused and picked up the flowerpot and scooped the soil back in, balancing the round-faced flowers on top of the soil, avoiding my eye. 'She isn't always very happy.'

'Oh,' I said, embarrassed that I had never asked before.

'But you see, with this system, if she wants people to knock, she can switch the green light on, and if she doesn't, she can put the red light on.' He pulled on the wires so that the switches slithered out from behind the door.

'But how will the old people and the milkmen and the other people know what the lights mean?'

He looked at me coldly. 'Everybody knows. It's electricity. It's obvious.' He took the switches back into the house and then turned back, a conciliatory swivel. 'Do you want to see my crystal radio?'

I shrugged uncertainly. He stepped into the house nonchalantly and I leapt off the gate, taking flat flakes of maroon with me on the seat of my shorts. The hallway was dark and velvety. There were heraldic patterns that I traced with my fingers as Brendan led the way up the stairs, still carrying his box. He opened his bedroom door and a buzzer went off quietly somewhere in the room. He held the door at arm's length and hopped gracefully into the room, landing on one foot and spinning his spare arm. There were wires and springs everywhere. Books lay open on the floor as if they had been shot in the back. I followed him in, letting the door shut behind me. The buzzer stopped.

'It's a burglar alarm,' he explained.

We hopped grandly around the wires until we reached a space on the floor next to his bed. He dragged a cardboard tube wrapped tightly in green wire from his pillow and held a small speaker next to my ear which fuzzed when he clipped a stray wire to the board. He turned the knob on the board in front of him until the humming tightened into a man's voice and I was able to make out words, then phrases and whole sentences. I looked up at Brendan in surprise and he nodded.

That was the moment when Brendan Hardcastle's influence over me was complete. Until then I had been unable to capture what it was that made him seem so much older than me, but when I heard the fuzzing voice coming out of the tiny speaker that he held between his finger and thumb, suddenly I understood. He had found a world of wires and buzzers and batteries, and had captured a small part of something bigger than himself, something that flew around our heads and to which I had been oblivious until now.

He gave me some clips and a book and a handful of wires to take home. I hopped out of his room and strode along the wall at the back of our houses until I was standing above my yard. I climbed down carefully, suddenly wary of dropping my new tools, tools that were to bring me into the bigger world that I had glimpsed that morning.

The first thing I made was a burglar alarm like Brendan's, with tin foil and wires and a battery that ran out when I forgot to shut my door before leaving for school. And a small circuit with a tiny bulb and an OR gate, so that I could turn it on at the switch that I stuck on the wall by the door and turn it off as I lay in bed. I made one of these for my mother but the bulb lasted for such a long time that I began to doubt her appreciation of it. And I made a circuit with a buzzer, so that when you tapped a lever the buzzer went off. This was made under Brendan's instructions so that together we could learn the intricacies of Morse, sitting on the wall above Brendan's yard, our buzzers on our laps and our batteries in our pockets, and Brendan reading aloud from a book. Like pilots, I thought.

So you see, it was because of Brendan that I learnt how to kick a football with the side of my foot and avoid complete ostracism. It was because of him that I paid attention in science classes and decided to be an electrician. It was because of him that I sloped silently to City and Guilds evening classes with my books under my jumper, avoiding my dad's swishing tail and the sign above the dairy that declared Royston and Son, newly singular. And really, it was because of him that I avoided being issued with the same one-way foot passenger ticket to Belgium that all the other boys from St Francis's School, Southwark, received.

On the day that war was declared, Stevie and I went to the pictures to watch the news in the afternoon. She fell asleep on my shoulder, her back aching from lifting sand and a sugared mouse melting in her hand. She twitched in her sleep, waking herself up as her head fell forwards, and then she turned drowsily to me as the newsreel showed soldiers from the advance British Expeditionary Force lining up to board a ship to France, kitbags slung over their shoulders. She kissed my cheek. 'You're too soft for this,' she murmured.

I didn't know what she meant. I rubbed my hand against my stubbled cheek. 'What do you mean, soft?'

'Delicate. Just skin and flesh.' She paused and brushed the base of my neck with her fingers. 'Like this bit. It would break so easily.'

I felt the place her fingers had touched. I felt the pulse beating in my neck, glands under my skin. I pictured veins and arteries stretching across my body, drawn in blue and red. I saw the men flickering in front of me, waving from the sides of the ship. 'But I have to go,' I whispered.

'I know,' she replied, matter-of-factly. 'Of course you do. That's not what I meant.'

'Oh,' I said.

'You should ask Brendan,' she said quietly, as the lights were dimmed yet further in readiness for the main feature. 'He'll know what to do.' She put her head back on my shoulder as the music began and I felt her body slacken against me once more as her breathing deepened. I put my arm around her and buried my nose in her hair.

The next day, I went to the maroon door and knocked and knocked until the red light was switched off and Brendan's mother opened the door and I saw that her lipstick was smudged over her teeth and her eyes were not quite dry.

'He's not here but you can wait in there.' Her voice was Scottish and gentle.

I jiggled on the settee for two hours. When Brendan got back he looked at me and saw my foot tapping against the ground.

'I thought you'd come,' he said, shaking off his coat and hanging it on the back of the chair. He made us both a cup of tea and then sat down and turned on the radio, adjusting the tuner until the sound came in a clear line instead of a cloud. A man was talking in an aching monotone about Polish resistance.

'Are you signing up?' I asked.

He nodded. 'Royal Signals,' he said. 'Much safer. Fewer guns.'

I nodded. I had not thought of that. 'When shall we go?'

'Tomorrow. I'll knock for you in the morning.'

We went for a beer and then I went home and sliced my neglected football against the wall until it was too dark to see and I could hardly stand. And I thought about Stevie as I got into bed, of how her hair smelt like shortcake mix, and I thought that I would ask her to marry me when I got back.

Stevie

Michael taught me to swim in the summer of 1939. The factory canteen closed at midday on Saturdays after the weekly deep-clean, and he would be waiting for me at the gates when I came out. He stood always in the same spot, next to a bush heavy with aphids, scribbling notes in one of Brendan's small yellow notebooks. They had hundreds of those small books, Michael and Brendan, filled with codes and pictures of wiry connectors, with symbols that I did not understand. Sometimes Michael would explain his diagrams to me, talking in a different, more serious voice as he showed me how to make temporary magnets and small buzzers. I would nod appreciatively and leap to attention when he issued instructions, holding wires for him while he screwed them in place, rubbing the hooves of my shoes against each other until he had finished, and wondering whether he had been born with an ear that looked as if it had a bite taken out of it, or whether something had happened to make it like that.

On Saturday afternoons, Michael and I would get the bus down to the Peckham Lido. It had been my idea. My arms ached from reaching for saucepan lids and pouring pots of boiling water into huge, vegetable-filled vats, and I was tired of standing on tiptoes with prickling eyes as I chopped onions. My head hurt from having to scrape my hair back so tightly into a hairnet that my ears pulled towards each other around the back of my head, their outer edges almost touching. I wanted to lie back and stretch my arms above my head and feel nothing at all beneath me.

There were cubicles around the edges of the pool with brightly coloured doors and soggy benches that dripped with discarded hairs. There were no roofs to the cubicles so I covered myself with a towel as I changed into Vivien's old swimming suit and bathing cap, embarrassed by the birds who sat on the tops of the splintery walls, watching the sun as it landed on my bare skin.

Michael was in the water by the time I emerged from my cubicle, floating amongst a mass of careless arms and legs belonging to other people's children. He looked longer and flatter when he was underwater. I padded towards him, my towel slung awkwardly over my shoulder. The swimming suit billowed around my breasts and sagged at my stomach, misshapen with thumbprints where I had tried to arrange it over my body. I felt his eyes on me, looking for the places where I bulged and softened. I folded my arms awkwardly across my chest like ironed shirtsleeves and stood on the tiles at the side of the bath.

'Is it cold?' I asked him.

He grinned at me and dipped his head into the water. His nose was blue when it came up. 'It's freezing,' he said happily, and then added, 'It's easier if you jump. I'll catch you.'

I was not sure about this. The water was deep and colourless and I decided that this might not be the best way to begin. I went sideways down the steps instead, immersing myself toe by toe. My skin prickled with the cold. Michael watched me as I edged towards him, my hands gripping the drain on the wall. He took my hand and rested it on his shoulder, pulling me away from the side of the bath, and then he told me to kick my legs while he swam in front of me, his body holding me up. I felt the warmth of his skin where it touched mine, the muscles moving in his back. I clung precariously to him, breathing into his neck and kicking my legs so that we would not drown. Gradually I grew accustomed to the shuddery motion of front crawl and the slow churning of breaststroke. Even when I no longer needed his help, I pretended that I did. I liked feeling his body underneath mine, my hands on his sides. I lowered my nose into his hair and allowed my stomach to bump against his back.

When we grew tired we stopped at the deep end and clung to the side of the pool. He told me to turn over and lie completely flat, his hand supporting the small of my back and my ears filling with water. We let out our breaths in large, slow bubbles as we sank to the bottom of the pool. His arms were bumpy and wide and distracting. I felt his hands brushing against my stomach, and my lungs emptied in a large and shimmering rush of air and I thought I might drown.

We stayed in the pool for hours that first time, until our legs draggled like seaweed and I could no longer lift my arms from the water. My hair shivered on my head and my fingers were beginning to ferment.

He was waiting for me on the steps outside the pool when I emerged from my booth, bleached white and waterproof. My neck was towel-dried and hot as we splashed along the path to the road.

'Are you hungry?' he asked.

My stomach growled in response. I was always hungry in those days.

He put his arm around me. I slipped mine around his back and up the inside of his jumper. His skin was smooth and warm under my wrinkled fingers. He steered me into the park and we climbed through a hole in the bushes, cracking the ground beneath us. We stopped when we came to two large stones under a thorny tree at the edge of the lake. The stones had round dips in the middle and we sank into them, exhausted.

Michael took from his bag two packets of sandwiches, wrapped in shiny paper. He handed one to me. 'These are yours. You said you didn't like butter in sandwiches so it's just straight corned beef.' He grinned at me. 'You see, I remember things.' He began to eat a buttery sandwich from the other packet.

I thought that was a promise, so I opened my mouth wide and savoured every second of it, deciding not to mention that corned beef gave me an itchy rash on my stomach.

I arrived home late that night. Vivien was sewing silently next to the clock in the front room, stitching a zip onto a bag. She smiled thinly at me as I came in. I kissed her head with my cheek and sloped upstairs, slithering into the bed I shared with my sister. That night I dreamt of bumpy arms and butterless sandwiches, and ears with bites taken out of them which, as it transpired, was a genetic characteristic. I imagined thumbprints on my body. I woke up with my hands gripping the side of the bed, trying not to fall out.

Michael

My father was a fastidious sleeper. He slept with his nose pointing to the swelling patch of damp in the corner of the ceiling and with his hands clasped together. He lay in this position as he prayed loudly for the benefit of both of us, one eye open so that he could check I had my eyes shut, and when he had finished he would lift his head on its rubbery neck and blow out the candle at an extraordinary angle.

He did not so much snore as hiss, his lips pressed tightly shut and the hairs whistling in his nostrils. He breathed so deeply that I grew dizzy if I tried to keep time with him. I felt his prayers rubbing coarsely against my skin, covering me like a rough blanket that itched every time I moved. They crept up my neck and blew against my face. They danced around me in the dark. I tried counting sheep, but they bared their teeth as they jumped over the gate and I saw that they were nothing but the woolly-coated false prophets of whom my father liked to whisper last thing at night. I found it impossible to sleep.

He would shush me if I moved in my bed. He would follow me if I went to the toilet in the night. I would find him standing at the back door looking blankly at the wall in front of him, waiting for me to scuttle back across the yard in my bare feet. He didn't say anything, but just followed me back upstairs and slinked back into Ben's narrow bed next to mine and resumed his breathing.

As I got older he told me that it was because he loved me. I found this sentiment unlikely. His eyes were still as glacial as they had been when Ben was alive, and yet there he was, every night, watching over me in case I too slipped quietly and hotly away in the night as my brother had done.

The nights were darker then. We had flickering bulbs that we rarely used, preferring candles and small gas lamps. The softness of the light hid the imperfections of the skin, and so we had not seen the depth of the rash covering Ben's face that night, and we had no inkling that when he slipped into a feverish sleep it was something stronger that pulled him from us, a huge great purple tentacle wrapped thickly around his ankle which pulled him down so deep he would never wake up.

Uncle Billy gave me a photograph he had taken of Ben and me in that last summer. I remember how I took it from his hand and pressed it grubbily to my heart and that, as I held it there, I was hit by the realisation that Ben had left me forever and this small image was all I had left of him. I remember how my father reached out and took the treasured photograph from my hands with his long fingers and brought it close to his face to look at it. He went to the kitchen and took a pair of scissors from the drawer next to the sink. He ran the soft pad of his fingertip along the blades and then scraped them against the round whetstone on the windowsill, and when he was satisfied with their sharpness he held the scissors up to the photograph and made a sharp cut through the middle of it.

So it is forgivable that most people think that the photograph on the wall above the fireplace is just of Ben. And that he is smiling at the camera.

But he wasn't. He was smiling at me.

He had bright blond hair that produced a strange photographic effect against the dark smudginess of the house behind him, so that his head seemed to be emanating light. His eyes were narrowed against the sun in a way that made him look older than his eleven years. His eyebrows were creased into a frown and he was wearing a white shirt and a red tie that looked grey in the photograph, and a rusty sheriff's badge in the shape of a star. Uncle Billy took the picture without warning us. I remember. Ben turned to look at him just as he pressed the button, and his mouth was still smiling from when he had been looking at me.

I was wearing green shorts on my head that day. The holes for my legs were folded in on themselves, wrapped around my head and tucked in at the sides. The metal button dug into my forehead, and a red feather was pinned precariously to the waistband of the shorts. My Robin Hood phase had lasted for nearly the whole summer of my eighth year and the red feather boa, purloined from a brown paper bag hidden under my mother's Sunday shoes in her cupboard, was becoming thin and stringy.

If you looked closely, you could see the small head of my arrow pointing at Ben, just at the edge of the photograph, made of brown rubber so that it wouldn't take anyone's eye out.

And if you looked closer still, you could see the white line running down the side of the photograph where it had been cut in half, as if struck by lightning. Clean in two. Except for that little triangle on the end of my arrow.

It was the only photograph ever taken of the two of us together. He died a few weeks after that sunny afternoon, so quietly that it was almost impossible to believe it had happened. I had always imagined death would be noisier.

Everyone started calling him Benedict as soon as he wasn't there to say that he didn't like it. Benedict. It made him sound like a syrupy medicine.

I remember my father looking at me in surprise as he laid the scissors carefully back in the drawer, as if I were a cow he had forgotten to milk. He went into the back room and propped the picture of Ben against the wall above the fireplace.

So that was when I was removed from the photograph, sliced carefully and deliberately, like a bruise from a banana.

I looked for my half of that photo on the night before I left for training but it had disappeared from the sideboard drawer. I wanted to give it to Stevie so that she would remember what I looked like while I was away. My mother had invited her for tea and we were pretending to be normal. My father refrained from his biblical musings, restricting himself to one frosty prayer. We talked about how the buses seemed jerkier in the blackout, and about how the iron railings had been taken from Trinity Church Square in the Borough.

After the meal, I walked Stevie home, detouring across

Peckham Rye. She was wearing a light green skirt that floated around her calves when she walked, and a white blouse with puffy sleeves. Her hair was in a knot at the back of her head, loose strands falling onto her neck. We climbed onto the wall at the back of her house to say goodbye. She turned to face me, her eyes as grey as socks, and she swung her legs over my knees.

I gave her the photograph of me in my uniform. She laughed at the way I had turned my shoulders to the side so that I didn't have to look straight at the camera. We had been given jackets with shoulder pads and hats that sat jauntily on the side of our heads. I remember looking along the line of men queuing up for a turn in front of the Baby Brownie camera and thinking that already we looked like a mantelpiece, a row of old photographs, resplendent in our sepia-coloured shirts and over-starched collars. We rubbed our boots on the backs of our trouser legs and smiled sternly. My mother put her copy of the photograph up above the fireplace next to the one of Ben, and my father nodded when he saw it, almost approvingly.

Stevie ran her finger gently over the picture of my face where it pressed flatly against the shiny paper. 'It looks like someone else,' she said quietly, and then lifted her hand to my cheek and turned me so that I was facing her. She put her arms around me and held the photograph behind my back between her finger and her thumb as if it were a fish that had gone off, and then she kissed me.

I was relieved that she could see the difference.

Stevie

My bedroom at Emily's house looks out over the garden. At night, I sometimes hear Anna climb onto her windowsill, one along from mine, and dangle her legs carelessly over the side. She wedges her back into the hinge of the glass and I hear a match being struck and a soft gulp of smoke. I don't remember when it happened, when she got so old. Nobody mentions her breasts. She still has child's hands, half-bitten and clammy to touch, but thin, grown-up arms and defiant knees.

She wants to be a doctor and it embarrasses her that I am so proud of her. I carry a photograph of her when she was five years old in my purse. She hates that photograph. It annoys her when I try to show it to people. She will understand, one day, when it is her granddaughter.

I move to the other end of the bed so that my head is by the window. I lie on my back, upside down, tipping my head backwards so that I can see out of the window. There are bats hanging calmly in the eaves above my head. They look as if they are standing up straight and balancing on tiptoes. I feel disorientated and let out a small hiccup.

Anna's voice comes floating in from the darkness. 'Nana? Is that you?'

'I was just having a look out of the window,' I whisper. 'There are bats above my head. Can you see them?'

Her cigarette fizzes as she stubs it out on the wall. 'I've seen them before. They're microbats,' she says.

'Oh.' I pause. Anna has a pedantic, scientific streak that is occasionally disconcerting. 'Is a microbat a bat?'

'Yes. It's just a sort of bat. A type. You can have macrobats as well, but they're not necessarily bigger. Just different. They eat different things.'

'Have you ever seen a bat eating?' I ask her.

She hesitates. 'No.'

'Are there any raisins downstairs?'

'I don't know. I'll go and have a look.'

She slides off her windowsill and flutters down to the kitchen. She knocks on my door before pushing it open, one hand curled protectively around a clump of raisins. I see her nose wrinkle slightly as she comes in and I wonder if I am making the room smell of old people.

We lean out and, with the metal nipple of my umbrella, I fetch one of the microbats a poke behind the ear. The bat gives a small shriek and begins to fly in circles, as if he has just seen a spider, and the other bats begin to rustle.

I start throwing raisins in loopy arcs.

'Nana, you're nowhere near them,' Anna sniffs loftily.

'Just wait.' I continue with my lobs.

'Have you ever done this before?'

'There, look.' A bat gobbles it up, nose-diving into the raisin with its mouth open, so that there is no tiny purple splatter on the patio below us this time. I throw another one, and we watch as another bat dives into it, gulping it just as it finishes its loop.

Anna steals a raisin from my hand and this time it is *her* raisin that gets swallowed up. She comes back into my room and starts throwing the raisins in the air, catching some of them in her mouth and losing the others among the tousled hairs of the carpet and under the bed.

'How did you know that they liked raisins?' She looks at me with a sudden curiosity.

'A friend of mine showed me.'

'Who?'

'Oh, someone I knew before the war.'

Anna looks at me. 'What happened to her?'

'Him. He went to Africa, and didn't come back.' I roll the raisins around my hand and try to avoid her eye.

Her eyebrows furrow as she looks at me. 'Did he die?'

'No,' I tell her. 'He just didn't come back. Well, he did come back eventually, but, well . . .' I hesitate. 'He was late.'

Anna turns slowly back to the window and throws a raisin. She is leaning out over the ledge, her hair blowing over her face. She turns back to me and smiles, and I notice the dip of her left ear.

I learnt about bats on the day before Michael left to go to the training camp. His mum had invited me round for tea and we ate cold slivers of fish that fell apart when prodded. I choked on a bone and the noise echoed off the plates that were hanging on the cream-painted walls of the kitchen, and bounced off the linoleum on the floor.

Afterwards, when it was already dark, Michael and I walked back across the park and he showed me how to feed raisins to bats. When we got to my house, we sat on the wall above the toilet shed at the end of the yard and he gave me a present, wrapped in pale blue tissue paper. Vivien's shadow was fluttering behind the curtain of my bedroom. I undid the paper, trying not to rip it, wanting to keep it after he had gone. It was a photograph of him dressed up as a soldier. He was baring his teeth in a forced attempt at a smile, but his eyes were glassy and nervous. His hair was greased so that it fell more heavily than usual over his right eye. I brushed the photograph with my finger, trying to smooth the hair out of his eye.

I turned to him abruptly. 'I love you.' I felt the words fall out of my mouth, hard-boiled and shiny, landing gently in my cupped palms. I felt myself spinning as my hands cradled the words. Don't laugh at me, I thought, please don't laugh.

He didn't laugh. He didn't even smile. His eyes were cloudy as he looked at me.

'Do you?'

I nodded. And waited. A brick wobbled under my leg.

And finally he held his hands out to me, and the spinning stopped as he pulled me close to him and held me tightly. He whispered it back to me as I pressed my head into his chest, so softly that I could only hear the words through the vibrations they made against the edges of his body. He said it three times. It sounded different when he said it. His words were runny and uncooked, slippery and transparent. I couldn't hold on to them. They seeped between my fingers and drenched my clothes. I rubbed them around my palms and into the backs of my hands.

Perhaps I should have guessed then that he might not mean what he said, but in those days I wasn't particularly fussy as to consistency. I hadn't realised it was important.

The night is quieter now. I lie back down in my bed, and imagine the bats lining up along the eaves, pulling their wings around them like eiderdowns and settling in for the night.

'Shall I shut the window?' Anna says after a while.

I nod. 'You should go to bed.'

'Alright. Night night, Nana,' she whispers, creaking out of the room and shutting the door laboriously quietly behind her.

'Goodnight, sweetie,' I murmur at her departing back.

The house is silent. Anna's window is shut. I can hear the bats snoring softly. Now there is only me. Still awake.

Michael

When I was fifteen, I learnt about black holes. I sensed them even before the teacher chalked a powdery white circle on the blackboard as we covered the basics of physics at evening classes and labelled the centre of it: *BLACK HOLE*. From an early age I had harboured a suspicion that the earth was slowly collapsing under its own gravity, being swallowed into an infinite centre, a centre so dense that not a single atom of light could escape. It was obvious to me because I was watching it happen to my mother. I saw her shrink infinitesimally smaller as my father towered over her. So it came as no surprise to me that this theory was generally applicable to all matter. I didn't see how it could have been other-wise.

As I grew older I began to feel the effects of gravity pressing down on my own head and flapping at the tips of my fingers. I felt the skin of my heels becoming loose and saggy and I wondered how long it would take for the process to become complete.

The war changed everything.

When the bombs began to fall, my father wrote to inform me that my mother had begun consorting with the Devil. He added this information as a postscript, neglecting to include any information as to the nature of their association.

It turned out that my mother had been going to the local underground shelter and singing songs she had never heard before whilst gulping small mouthfuls of gin from old bottles passed along the platform. My father refused to accompany her on these expeditions. He believed that if God wanted him to be kept safe, then He would keep the bombs away from him, and if it were God's will, then he would die in his own bed.

This was not a new theory. My father liked to apply this philosophy to every area of his life. He would walk into roads without looking for motor cars. He pushed us into ponds before we had learned to swim and watched us floundering with interest, as if it were a sophisticated experiment. He strode across railway lines with no thought for the timetable. As a child, I found him a terrifying guide.

During air raids, my father would remove all his clothes and fold them into a neat pile and lay them on the pillow next to him. He would get into his bed and shut his eyes, and mutter things like, 'Naked came I from the womb, and naked shall I return thither.' My mother would raise her eyes to the metal-filled skies and storm out of the house to the underground station, wrapped in blankets and wearing my father's rubber boots on her feet. And in the middle of each of the three nights that I was back home on leave from the training camp in Catterick, she would come to my room when the sirens went off and take hold of my hand and drag me sleepily behind her.

I remember how my father tried to stop us on the first

night, following us down the stairs and blocking the doorway. The lightbulbs in the hallway buzzed as his voice reverberated against them. I pulled on my coat and tried to hustle my mother out of the door, but the Devil had clearly got into her good and proper because, quite suddenly, she turned on the doorstep and looked at my father in a way that I had never seen before, and hissed her words so quietly that at first I wasn't sure that I had heard her. 'Just leave us alone.' Then she looked up and I knew she had said it because her eyes were wide and terrifying, and her neck looked like it was chipped out of stone. She reached for my hand and then she said it again, more loudly this time, so there could not be any doubt, and I felt the skin on my heels grow taut.

'Give it a rest, Simon. Leave us alone. Leave him alone.'

Just that. Nothing more.

She crossed her arms across her chest and looked at him, and I began to wonder if everyone had got Einstein the wrong way round. Perhaps we were not collapsing in on ourselves but moving constantly outwards. I had no equations to base this controversial theory on, no scientific evidence as such, just a sudden intimation of infinite expansion.

And what surprised me even more is that he did give it a rest. He stared at my mother and then began to edge quietly back up the stairs, his shoulders slumped against the wall, and my mother turned to me, her eyes as wide as if she had just found a pound note on the street. She took my arm and dragged me into the kitchen to show me how the back of the cupboard didn't quite touch the wall, and how you could swing the panel aside and run your hand along the skirting boards until you found the thin neck of a bottle of gin. She measured it out by pouring it into a tablespoon and then adding an extra drop, and then she drank it from a teacup made from china so thin it was almost transparent. She sipped it, screwing up her nose, as if she was drinking a cup of tea with sour milk. I tipped mine down all in one go, straight from my old orange beaker and felt it lying hotly against my throat. And then we ran to the shelter, hooting loudly.

The next day, after a strange tea of green-pea eggs with rice and raisins and a few more tablespoonfuls of gin, I went on my mother's bicycle to meet Stevie at the factory gate. The air smelt of stale peanuts, even though the factory now produced grey metal instead of Sun Pat spread. I saw her folding her apron into her bag and running her hand over her hair as she came towards me, tucking her blouse into her skirt, so that her body went in and then out again.

I had forgotten how short she was and how her nostrils flared slightly when she laughed. She felt so light when she jumped up and locked her legs around my middle to kiss me. She licked the gin from my lips, removing my protective layer so that my body began to tremor slightly. She didn't seem to mind the other girls laughing and tutting and turning their heads away, trying not to think of the boys I reminded them of.

Stevie sat on the handlebars facing me. My knees were poking out to the side like a grasshopper. We tacked bumpily to the Rye, wobbling with nerves on an elongated centre of gravity, distracted by the gap that lay between us. We cycled past the hay crops that had been planted in straight lines on the common, then past the bowling green and the lake, until eventually I gave up and tipped her gently from the handlebars so that she fell onto the ground, hands first, into a sheltered patch behind a tree. I fell next to her, and we lay on the grass feeling small and expectant.

'You're shaking.' She was looking at me, running her fingers along the lumps of my arm.

'Sorry.'

'You don't have to be sorry. It's fine.' She looked at me. 'Tell me.'

'Tell you what?'

'Tell me anything. Tell me about what you did in Catterick. Tell me what they were teaching you at the training camp. Anything.'

I wanted to impress her so I told her something Brendan had told me about the Hubble telescope, and about how people in America used to queue up to watch Edwin Powell Hubble at work, and how a girl called Mary had fallen in love with him as she stood on tiptoes, craning over another man's shoulder to see, and Hubble had spotted her and married her.

Stevie wrapped her arms around her knees and pulled them into her. She was shivering. I edged closer and leapt clumsily on to natural history as I put my arm across her shoulders, taking the migration of eels as a starting point and, when that topic was in danger of exhausting itself, I paused for a moment and she leant in towards me and kissed me. She held me tightly against her and, even though it was October, she opened a button of her blouse so that my face could lie in the warm dip of her chest.

On the next night, my last night, I went to meet her from the factory again and we walked hand in hand across the Rye as, in the distance, the bombs fell beautifully behind us. We lay on the grass, wrapped in coats and scarves. Fear of leaving made me restless and brave. I unbuttoned her coat and opened the button below the one she had allowed me the night before, never taking my eyes from hers, and then the next and the next. Her skin was hard and goose-bumpy, and smelt of disinfectant and cabbages. Her hands were in my hair. I pulled her skirt up over her hips, and she lifted her head in surprise. She put her hands flat against my chest as if she were going to push me away but then she paused, and as I looked at her she began to nod, slipping her hands around my back and pulling me on top of her.

Afterwards she looked away from me, suddenly shy. I kissed her neck as she buttoned up her blouse and tucked it back into her skirt. Her cheeks were red as she reached up to smooth down her hair. She turned to me suddenly, her hands reaching around me as she whispered, 'Tell me where you're going. I want to be able to look for you on the map.'

'Africa.' I said. 'They're sending me to Africa.'

'Africa?' She paused. 'Why?'

'The Italians are in Africa. We need to push them back up north.' I tried to sound nonchalant but I had looked up Africa on a map too, and Italy seemed quite a long way to push somebody. I imagined grimy palms pressed against each other, feet slipping, pushing and pushing.

Stevie wrinkled her nose and shrugged. 'It still seems so far away.'

'I know, but I'll be back. It's safer in Signals so I'll be

fine, and Brendan will be with me.' I kissed her, hoping that she might not see that I had no idea of what I was going to. 'I'll come back for you, I promise. I'm not going to leave you.'

She looked at me and rubbed her hands against each other. 'I'll be waiting,' she said, and began to do up the laces of her shoes. We stood up slowly.

I left the next morning while it was still halfway between darkness and light, detouring past her house to throw stones at her window so that she might lean out one last time.

'I love you.' Her words floated softly onto my upturned face, as delicate as snowflakes. I looked back from the end of the road and I saw a shivering silhouette of a girl in a baggy nightie still leaning out of a window, her arms folded protectively across her stomach. I could feel the softness where her kiss landed on my cheek for hours after it had melted.

Stevie

On the morning the Sun Pat was bombed, I was lying in bed and vomiting into a bucket.

Vivien came clattering in the front door. 'Stephanie! Stephanie! Where are you? Please, Stevie love, please be here!'

I lifted the hair away from my face and was trying to manoeuvre my feet to the floor when the bedroom door crashed open. 'Oh, my angel!' Vivien cried, launching herself at me. She grabbed my arms and pulled me from the bed and I collapsed against her.

'What's happened?' I asked, my face squashed into Vivien's bony bosom.

'The factory's on fire. It's been bombed. The fire escape went down and the streets are full of girls. I thought you might be in there.' She stopped and looked at me. 'Why aren't you in there?'

I gestured towards the bucket next to my bed. 'I've been sick.'

She nodded, and wiped a tear from her eye. 'The Lord moves in mysterious ways,' she announced dramatically, and then tucked me back into my bed and sat down to watch me until I fell asleep. I found out later that three of the canteen girls had been killed on the fire escape, porridgey spoons still in their hands, and their bodies were taken down the Old Kent Road on a dust cart.

The next day, I tied my hair into an officious bun, using a pencil to secure it in the hope that I would appear scholarly, and went to re-register at the Ministry of Labour. The pencil did the trick. A woman with white hair and gold spectacles watched as I filled in my details on the form, and then tilted her head and asked if I could spell 'business'. As I stood up to leave, she offered me a post as a receptionist at the Ministry of Labour office in Newington Butts, and I nearly burst with excitement.

I started the very next day. I wore a shirt with a collar that was the colour of notepaper, and an old pair of Vivien's shoes. I could feel the cracks of the pavement beneath my feet as I walked.

I had a desk of my own in a wood-panelled room with brass doorknobs, and a drawer full of forms that were to be filled in when people came to register for employment. Eva, the girl on the desk next to me, was bright and summery, with blonde hair that fell in soft curls around her flushed cheeks. She showed me where I was to file each completed form and where to put my scarf, and then sat at her desk and took out a small mirror and looked sideways at her reflection as the queue began to rustle in the hallway.

My first appointment was with a sooty woman who had lank hair and a stained navy blue overcoat. She grinned as she spoke, as if she knew something I didn't, which I realised later she probably did.

'Name.'

'Rita Seymour.' She smiled suggestively at me.

I wrinkled my forehead and tried to remain formal.

'Could I take the address of your last place of employment?'

'I ain't been employed. I were inside.'

'Inside where?'

' 'Olloway, of course. Where else? There's only one for women, ain't there?'

There was a short pause, while I struggled to understand. Rita began to roll a cigarette, her eyes watching me as she ran her tongue along the thin paper. Suddenly I remembered, and wrote *Holloway Ladies' Prison* in the appropriate box, adding the apostrophe with a satisfied flourish. 'And what was your trade before you went to prison?'

'Light Entertainment.'

I looked at her, slightly puzzled, and tried to imagine her on stage, make-up covering the bruises behind her eyes.

She leant in towards me and I smelt powdered egg on her breath. 'I'm a prostitute, Miss.'

'Oh,' I said nonchalantly. 'Of course.' I ran my finger down the list of categories, searching for the appropriate classification.

'There isn't a proper category for us. I been here before, see. They put us under Light Entertainment. Code E79.'

I looked uncertainly at Eva. She nodded encouragingly at me, and waved at Rita. 'Back again, eh Rita?'

Rita nodded. 'Let out for good behaviour, wasn't I? Stupidest thing I ever did.' She looked back at me. 'I wouldn't bother putting me in any factory, Miss. I'm going straight back inside as soon as December comes around. It's the best place to be at Christmas. I wouldn't miss it for all the tea in China.'

'Oh, I see.' I paused. 'The thing is, Miss Seymour . . .'

'Missus,' she corrected me.

'Sorry. What I mean to say, Mrs Seymour, is that I need some proof of your . . .' I hesitated, uncertain of the word.

'My profession?'

'Yes, that's it. Your profession.'

Rita sighed, and bent down to scrabble in her shoe, her scraggy cigarette dangling between her teeth. She produced a scrumpled note.

'What's this?'

'It's a receipt from the policeman who fined me yesterday. You've always got to ask for a receipt, Miss, just in case.'

I nodded in agreement, and took the receipt from her, smoothing it out and clipping it to her form. 'That'll do nicely,' I told her. 'I'll be in touch.'

As it was, nobody wanted Rita anyway. The factories wouldn't take her because they were full of upper-class girls who refused to share toilets with prostitutes, and the services wouldn't have them. By the time employment had been found for Rita, it was December and she was back in Holloway, as she had promised she would be, having kicked an unwary policeman in the shins on the first Sunday of Advent, and then jiggled impatiently in front of him while she waited to be apprehended.

I found that it was a relief to be out of the factory, away from chopping boards and boiling vats and the lingering smell of peanuts. I carried papers in neat piles under my arm and clipped the wings of my blouse together with an old brooch of Vivien's so that they covered my neck in what I imagined to be a teacherly fashion. My hands softened and my back stopped aching.

I wished Michael could see me like this. I told Eva about him over frosty sandwiches on a bench in Kennington Park, and she choked on her half-chewed mouthful of date jam and utility bread.

'What was it like?' she demanded, tapping her foot impatiently against the pavement and pawing at my elbow.

'It was slippery,' I told her thoughtfully. 'But nice.'

I became neat and prim. I wore clips in my hair every day and sewed a pocket onto my blouse so that I could carry pens in it. I tutted at the girls from the secretarial office who idled away in the washrooms for hours, warming their bottoms against the hot-water pipes, and who smiled knowingly at me when I emerged greenly and confusedly from my cubicle, nausea still whirling around my empty stomach.

It turned out that it was not just Rita who knew more than I did.

Michael

My photographs are on the table next to me, propped up against my vase. I hold them up to my eyes and squint at them. It is Alf's face that draws me in once again.

I have never told anyone about what happened to me in Africa in 1941. The events of that year are packed tightly inside me, squeezed against my edges so that they drip into my dreams at night like rising damp, marinading my mornings with guilt. There is so little time left. I take my notepad and start to write.

I met Alf on the boat out to Africa. We left from Liverpool, and various extensions of his curly-haired family crowded the dock to wave us off. We went the long way round to Africa as the Mediterranean was filled with Italians, and we set off across the Atlantic, tacking our way towards the Cape of Good Hope and pitching heavily as we went.

It was not long before it became apparent that Alf did not like the sea. He sat at the bottom of a long line of dockers. His dad and his granddad had both died at the docks, one being blown from a crane by a gust of wind, and the other suffering the more modern fate of being crushed by falling machinery. Alf had spent most of his

106

young life trying to avoid the sea, refusing walks with red-cheeked girls along the banks of the Mersey in favour of going home to his mam. In an attempt to stay on dry land, he had become apprenticed to an electrician with no teeth and burnt fingers who suffered from an uncanny knack for misconnecting earth wires. But try as he might, Alf could not escape the ocean. He spent large portions of each day leaning over the railings of the boat, looking at the waves rolling beneath him and retching with the wind so that it didn't blow back into his face, and wishing he had joined the RAF.

Brendan and I were fine whilst crossing the Atlantic. We would leave Alf outside at mealtimes and sit at long tables in the middle of the ship with the other servicemen who could stand the sight of food. We ate from cracked plates that slid from side to side along the table so you were never sure whose plate you were eating from by the time they had slithered back to your end of the table.

We rounded the Cape, and headed up through the Mozambique Channel, ploughing through the Indian Ocean along the eastern side of Africa. The ship now rolled instead of pitched and it was Brendan and I who found ourselves licking our fingers to check the direction of the wind before leaning over the railings, while Alf went into the dining room in search of food.

There was something comical about Alf that drew me to him. He was tall and thin and allergic to the sea air, and he announced with a grin on the third day that he had developed itchy piles. His nose began to bleed and would not stop, leakages that he believed to be dictated by the movements of the atmospheric isobars. His eyes dripped salty tears onto the pile of cards that he held in his lap during the interminable card games we played on the deck. Pools of saliva encrusted his pillow.

He found it impossible to sleep in the heat of the poorly ventilated lower cabins, and he would nudge me awake, with a whispered 'Mick, Mick, gerrup and come with me'. Nobody had ever called me Mick before. Together we would drag our mattresses up the stairs and onto the decks and be gently rocked to sleep under the stars until the boy with the slosh bucket woke us at dawn, and then we would bump our sodden mattresses back down the narrow stairs to the bunkroom for the day.

The voyage took forty-one days. We emerged dizzily, two by two, with red peeling noses and thin bodies exuding sweat and boredom. Our shirts were stiff with salt and ragged in places where we had dangled them from sticks over the side of the boat to wash them. On disembarkation, we were each given three tins of sardines and some salty bread and then we were left under a patch of palm trees, hiding from the sun. We did not know how long these rations were to last us. A small native man with no teeth climbed up the trunk of one of the trees that grew at a gentle angle to the ground, resting his feet in the slatted axe-marks that went all the way up. He showed us how to chop the top off the coconuts without spilling the contents, and the juice was sourly refreshing. That night, we slept on the dusty platform at the train station, and left before the sun had risen.

We took the train as far as Nakuru, a dirt track masquerading as a town high along the edge of the Great Rift Valley. For a few weeks I was posted in a radio hut in the grounds of a deserted European primary school.

My chair was so low that even tapping my foot in time to the sound of the messages coming through was uncomfortable.

There was an old Swahili Bible in one of the classrooms and Alf and I spent hours scanning through for familiar passages. We guessed the meanings of words and wrote them down on the blackboard of our classroom, later testing them out on the *totos* who lived in our camp, small Kikuyu boys who washed our clothes and wore our caps and drilled each other in the empty courtyard of the school. They would cheer encouragingly as we spoke to them in our stilted and biblical Swahili, and they would argue among themselves about what we had been trying to say.

Alf sat in the partition next to mine, both of us sending and receiving messages that arrived without warning over the huge radios we had set up in wooden boxes. We spoke to tank commanders already heading north, oblivious of the click that awaited them. We translated commands into capital letters and tapped them out to send to other battalions. We wrote reports of ill-timed attacks in lower case and stamped out requests for machinery in formal fonts. And we sent home sombre lists of the dead, finishing each message, as instructed, with the command: ... – . – *Stet*. Let it stand. There is no more.

Our telegraph lines would go down every few days and Alf and I would set off in the truck to find where they had broken. Usually it was a deliberate cut. We would see camels passing us days later, bundles tied to their backs with snipped telegraph wire and we would try to explain that the wire needed to be left alone, but we would be greeted only with innocent smiles and coconuts, and the replacement wire would be cut again a few days later when the need arose.

It was the night shifts that I liked best. I liked the solitude of them, the peacefulness of being alone on the line while Alf muttered in his sleep in the tent, and I liked the depth of the sky at night as the line buzzed faintly next to my ear. We formed a line across Africa, us men in our small huts resting sleepily next to our radios. Some nights we would chatter away when the line was quiet. I learnt to tell who was signalling to me just by the way they sent their dots and dashes. There was one signaller called Bobby, who hummed his dashes and tripped his dots as if he were playing the jazz piano, and another called Andy who dropped his 'g's and 'h's. We watched the sky and swatted at mosquitoes and we waited and waited.

During the day, things went back to normal. We would try to catch each other out, sending messages too fast to be comprehensible so that the recipient would have to ask for a repeat. The request would come back reluctantly and the network would buzz with Os and Hs which, when translated into Morse, sounded almost like laughter, and the sender would repeat the message at an agonisingly slow rate. Eventually I learned to transmit at an average speed of twenty-three words per minute, which was faster than Brendan and I had ever managed on that wall in my backyard, and fast enough to occasionally require a repeat. Alf was never as fast as me. He was more deliberate, a perfectionist.

We stayed at the school for just over two months, while the rest of the platoon finished digging the trenches along the Tana River. Brendan had been sent to Nairobi to help repair the old communications wires left over from the last war, so it was only me and Alf staying at the school. We took it in turns to swim each morning, the non-swimmer standing at the side and watching for crocodiles through the viewfinders of the rifles we hardly knew how to use. We played football against the walls of the school, and I showed Alf all the things that Brendan had taught me. Alf told me how his dad had taken him to see Everton every week when he was little, balancing him on a toolbox so that he could see over the caps of the men in front of him. He told me about his favourite player when he was a boy, a man called Dixie Dean who thumped his forehead so hard against the ball that nobody could stop it once it had left his head, and then he told me that his dad used to take him to the park and throw balls at him on Sundays. He would come home with a muddy forehead and no memory of the day before, and his mam would curse Dixie Dean under her breath, muttering that no one would ever employ a boy who couldn't remember what he'd had for breakfast from one day to the next.

We practised thumping the ball with our heads every day, and we spent the evenings analysing our progress as we sat next to the fire. The nights buzzed with small animals and the sky lay thickly over the school huts. And much later, while Alf dreamt of his dad's arms lifting him up to see Dixie Dean, I would shut my eyes and dream of Stevie.

Stevie

'Nana!' Anna calls from upstairs. 'Have you finished my dress?'

'Just a minute, sweetie.' I push my foot onto the pedal of the sewing machine, holding my breath as the needle eats at the soft purple silk. Next to me on the table is Vivien's old sewing box, stuffed with old cottons and scrumpled sewing patterns. I pull the material away from the needle and cut the threads, holding the dress in front of me as I eye it dubiously.

Dress-making has never been a particular strength of mine. It is the sort of skill that skips a generation. Vivien's creations were practical and streamlined. Mine had unruly hems and sagging waists and were generally reworked by Vivien to such a degree that I stopped making any effort at all.

Anna comes in and kisses me on the head. 'Thank you. It looks great.'

I am not so sure. 'Try it on first.'

'I've got ages yet.' She sits at the table next to me, pulling idly at the patterns in the sewing box, unfolding them and spreading them across the table. I watch her uncertainly.

She picks one up and laughs. 'Listen to this one.' She

affects a posh accent and reads aloud. '*The quaint padded effect on the bodice and sleeves is easily achieved by shirring and is particularly becoming to the too slim.* Is that yours, Nana?'

I take the pattern that she is holding out to me. 'Yes.'

'Why were you making a dress like that?'

'Oh, it was probably for a dance. During the war,' I reply vaguely.

She looks suddenly suspicious. 'Were there lots of dances during the war?'

'Yes.' I fold the pattern over abruptly.

'Is that how you met Granddad?'

'I met your granddad at the Ministry. He was an inspector. You know that, don't you?'

She shrugs. 'I forgot. I thought you worked in a factory.'

'I did. But it got bombed.'

'Oh.' She takes her dress and holds it against her shoulders, swinging it around her. 'It looks great. Thank you.'

Perhaps I have improved over the years. 'You should go and get ready,' I tell her.

She nods grudgingly but doesn't move. She is reluctant to go to the party, I have guessed that much, although she refuses to talk about it. The exams have finished and they will all be talking about universities and what they will be doing next. Anna is not going to university because Scott would not allow her to apply. He said that she should work for a few years first, claiming it would be better for her career, although really it is because he does not want to pay anything for her. He has always been mean, that man.

I put my hand on her arm. 'We can sort something out,' I say, 'about university. If you want to go . . .'

113

Anna looks at me and shrugs. 'It's not important. I don't need to go now. I can train as a nurse in a few years. It'll be fine.'

I feel an ache in my chest that she will not allow her disappointment to show. 'Anna, it is important. It's important to me.'

She smiles at me and stands up, shaking her head. 'I don't want to talk about it,' she says, and leaves the room, her footsteps heavy on the stairs.

I open up the old pattern again. I do remember that dress. I remember the folds of cloth that protruded from my armpits and burrowed upwards into my neck. I remember the resentment I felt at the way the pattern had oversimplified the ease with which the desired padded effect could be achieved. I thought that perhaps the fabric was wrong. Even when I tried swinging around as abruptly as I could, I still couldn't make it swish the way it did in the pencilled drawing next to the instructions.

The pattern had suggested taffeta or chiffon, fabrics that lay stretched out in snooty pre-war rolls of bright blue and pink on the top shelf of Abbott's, unattainable even before the war. I had to resort to Vivien's wardrobe, where I found an old dress I remembered her wearing when my dad was alive. The material was formal and intricate, maroon with red swirls, stiff as a dead rabbit. I tried it on, following the instructions implied by the abundance of buttons and clips that ran around the outside edges of the offending garment, clipping it tightly to my neck and clamping the sleeves around my wrists so that it was impossible to bend my elbows. Vivien had laughed when she found me and handed me a pair of shearing scissors.

'Start with the arms,' she suggested.

I bought the pattern from Helen. Helen worked in the secretarial office at the Ministry and had been to boarding school in the West Country from an early age and had developed an extra-loud voice to compensate for this fact. She was irreverently excited about the American soldiers who had started to roam the streets of London, and had taken up with a black soldier who was posted in Lambeth, the location of which only seemed to add to the exoticism of the whole affair in Helen's eyes. She would make cryptic comments about his anatomy as she powdered her nose at the end of a shift, and the rest of us would smile and try to avoid her eye in the mirror. The week before the dance, she stuck a poster up on the wall next to the kettle in the ladies' washroom, advertising sewing patterns. She had paid the extortionate fee of 9d to a mail order service for a new pattern and was now attempting to make a profit from this initial outlay by charging 1d to every girl she lent the pattern to. The pattern claimed to suit everyone because most of us now counted in the ranks of the too-slim after thirteen months of wartime rationing.

I remember how I tried on the dress the day before the dance, standing on the patch of carpet in front of the mirror, worn thin by vanity. It was tight around my waist so I loosened it at the back, slipped it off my shoulders and let it fall to the floor. It landed dustily at my feet and I ran my hands critically over my stomach, inspecting it, warming it softly with my hands.

I stood there in a daze, while the rest of my body slowly turned transparent as the cold seeped upwards from my feet.

So, really, I suppose I must have already known.

Michael

You see, Anna, this is something you will learn. What I tell you is true, in the way that only science can be true, stripped of words that complicate and confuse.

Anna smiles. 'Go on.' She rolls me onto my side and whips the sheet out from underneath me. I feel her fingers digging into my skin, holding me there, one shoulder suspended above the bed, while she aligns the new sheet against the mattress.

I wonder how else I can put it.

Her grip loosens on my arm and I roll back onto my pyramid of pillows. She smooths the sheet down over my legs and tucks it around my middle, and then stands with her hands on her hips, waiting for me to explain.

I draw a diagram, scribbling labels and adding arrows to show the directions of particles of light when a torchlight is directed through a hole in a piece of cardboard. She watches my pencil as it shudders over the paper.

What I want to tell her is this. There is scientific proof that our existence is not predestined to be smooth. Microscopic studies of matter show that, when you break it down, light comes in both waves and in particles,

117

landing upon us in ripples and pricking us with tiny dots. Light is not continuous, even though it may appear to be so. We do not bathe in sunlight, but shower in it.

Of course, we have filtering systems inside ourselves, creating the illusion of a smooth progression from one reality to the next. But this is not how it really happens. Reality does not creep up on us. It does not exist in a straight-line graph at the peak of which we react proportionately and appropriately to the circumstances that have propelled us there. Instead, it lurches towards us, catching us off-guard, and landing in our stomachs like a clenched fist before we have had time to tense our muscles against it. This is the ultimate lesson of quantum physics.

Do you see what I am trying to say, Anna?

She looks up from the scribbles in my notebook and screws up her nose. 'Not really.'

I crumple up my diagram and throw it towards the bin. I need to be more linear.

Our orders came through to start the push into Somaliland in the first week of 1941. We followed the Tana River eastwards and crossed at Bura, heading to the straight edge of Kenya. We waited there for six days. The land on the Somali side was patchy and brown and the border was marked with lines of barbed wire. It was a measure of the depths of our reluctant boredom that a discussion started by Alf regarding the probable number of barbs of wire in a certain section of the line was not greeted with disdain but became a favoured topic of conversation. We sat in the thick bush of Kenya and looked vacantly at the linen maps we had been given.

There were vast expanses of optimistically blank cloth that marked the land we were to pass through.

Once we reached Somalia, we had one bottle of water each per day. I had never known dryness like it. We passed through the Ogden desert and the dust seeped into our skin and hair, circling our eyes and settling in our ears. The Sappers went first, on motorbikes with hooks that dug into the ground to lift Italian mines from the ground. Kismayu, Mogadishu, Jigjiga, Harrar. We wrote the names onto our maps as we passed through.

Our skin became blotchy with mosquito bites, and the truck was feverishly hot. We took turns driving, delirious with thoughts of hospitals and squashed insects and the sound of water. The land became more mountainous as we approached Addis Ababa. The Italians blew up the roads behind them, and we spent hours filling up impassable holes with empty petrol drums and soil until they could hold the weight of the convoy.

On the whole, we saw very little of the Italians. We heard a rumour that they were planning on marching triumphantly into Abyssinia to the strains of *Aida*, and one of our other divisions claimed to have come across a storeroom of sheet music and ceremonial dress for the occasion. It was hard to know what to make of an enemy such as that.

We were nearly at Addis Ababa when it happened.

It was raining for the first time in months, heavy, tropical rain that landed loudly on the sagging canvas of our tents. The air buzzed with sandflies that the *totos* captured and devoured as if they were some sort of delicacy, first removing the wings and then the feet, and then dropping the body into their mouths.

'Everyone shut up. The Italians are over there. We're surrounded.'

The whisper ran round the camp. Feet rustled like frightened leaves. We smelt tobacco smoke floating towards us, thickening the clouds that lay protectively between us, waiting for morning.

We stopped setting up the camp and sat in silence in the rain. I gathered my knees neatly around my body and waited. I could feel fear being dipped into me like a teabag, pinched between grubby fingernails and swirled carelessly, turning my insides gradually darker, until the darkness had sunk deeper inside me and I could no longer see the bottom. Eventually I fell asleep, whispering half-remembered prayers to myself as my clothes clamped themselves heavily into the contours of my body.

'Is this true?' Anna says, looking up from my notebook. I nod dismissively, and indicate that she must read on. I lie down in my bed and turn my face away from her as she reads.

I remember every second of that night. It was still dark when I woke up. My uniform was as cold as a snail. I reached for the last of my rations, prising my coat apart and searching for the pocket of my uniform. I raised the flask in my hands to my lips, letting the liquid drip into my mouth. The sharpness of the whisky surprised me, and it sank into the gaps between my teeth and nestled in the ridges in the roof of my mouth. Alf was lying next to me. I nudged him and passed him my flask. I heard him groan softly as he sat up, jiggling his legs as he rummaged in his bag for his mug.

'Are they still there?' he asked.

'I don't know.' The rain was loud and heavy.

I felt a hand clamping on my arm. Alf jumped next to me and let out a small shriek. ''kin' 'ell, Royston!' hissed the captain. 'What do you think you're doing, making all that racket?'

'Sorry, sir.'

'It was me, sir,' Alf said.

'No, it wasn't him, sir . . .' I tried.

'I don't care who it was. Both of you, come with me. I've got a special mission.' Captain Williams dragged us roughly by our elbows and led us to the edge of the enclosure. His legs were as long and thin as rifles, and his knees clicked when he walked. Alf was still half-asleep. His confused body knocked against my arm as he stumbled next to me.

The captain stopped suddenly, and held his finger to his lips. 'Over there,' he whispered. 'They're sleeping. You, Royston, stay here. Watch our backs. Hooper, you're coming with me.'

Alf looked nervously at me and fumbled for his gun.

'Not that, idiot. You'll wake everyone,' the captain snapped. 'Your knife.'

Alf's hand trembled as he reached into the pouch in his sock. The rain was crashing around us. I heard the captain hissing instructions to Alf. Once across the throat. Deep and fast. Alternate men. Not all of them. Just get enough of them. Every other one.

'I can't,' Alf said, his voice shaking. 'I can't do that.'

'You walk away, lad, and I'll shoot you at dawn. I'll shoot you myself.'

I turned my back to them and shut my eyes. I pressed

my gun into my shoulder, and pretended to myself that I could not hear.

I look across at Anna and I see her mouth fall slightly apart as she reads.

Alf came back with salty rain streaming down his face and blood covering his hands and boots. The captain would not look at me. He put his hand on Alf's shoulder, and I heard him say, 'Good lad, Hooper. Good work.'

I avoided Alf's eyes and we returned to the rest of the platoon in silence. I remember, as clearly as if it were yesterday, looking down at the pattern that my boot left under the trees as we walked back, round and toeless and covered in tessellating patterns with ridges like claws around the edges.

We arrived in Addis Ababa at lunchtime. We drove our trucks straight to the hospital and lined up, baring our buttocks to the fierce nurse with her quinine injections. It was a relief to lie in that noisy hospital bed, feeling the fever wash over me and take me down with it so that I no longer had to think of Alf's face and what he had done, and what I had let him do because I didn't want to have to do it myself.

Stevie

The Ministry of Labour dance was held on a blitzy night at the beginning of February.

'Stevie! I didn't think you'd come! Come and dance with me. You can be the girl.'

I looked up at Eva. She was dressed all in blue with pale satin ballet shoes, and her lips were tinted pink.

'I still don't feel very well,' I said, parting the fog inside my head to get the words out.

Eva looked disappointed.

'Oh, one dance won't hurt, I suppose,' I said, standing up and taking the chair with me by mistake. My feet were bare. I had discarded my too-small brown shoes under a chair as soon as I had arrived, kicking them together so that their heels were touching and the bump in the leather where my big toe had been was soft and airy. Eva led me in a sideways gallop from one end of the hall to the other, avoiding the overflow of girls who leant self-consciously against the flaking walls. We clasped our hands together and held them out in front of us like a joust as we wove around the other dancers, unsteady with laughter.

The music was bellowing in my ear. It felt like it was being force-fed through a tube. I was suddenly dizzy with colour. Pinched cheeks and spinning skirts confused me. Thin arms bounced off me. The smell of camomile swishing in ponytails made me feel sick. I longed for grey flannel to catch me but there were no men, only a few soft-skinned boys with long arms and smooth cheeks.

My legs folded like empty white pillowcases.

I woke up on the floor of the toilet. Faces were climbing over each other to look at me and Eva was patting my head with a wet tissue. There was a pain drawn in a straight line across my stomach. And the blood on my dress was bright red. Not safe, brown blood. Red, living blood.

And that was when I knew for certain.

The blood had stopped coming by the time the doctor arrived in a car with two mattresses strapped to the roof to protect against shrapnel. His car had only one window and a cracked windscreen, and he was wearing a green cravat and a patchy black coat. He shooed everyone out of the bathroom and took my temperature. I wanted him to do something more dramatic. I wanted injections, bandages, medicines in brightly coloured bottles, but he merely prodded me and put his ear to my stomach and eventually said that it was just a bit of bleeding.

'Your baby is fine,' he told me, as he struggled to fit the unmatching buttons of his overcoat through holes that had been intended for smaller, more orderly buttons. 'You've just been overdoing it a little.'

'I'm pregnant?' I whispered.

He looked at me incredulously. 'Of course you are. Didn't you know?'

I shook my head, and then shrugged sheepishly. 'It had crossed my mind,' I mumbled. I was terrified, and suddenly very cold.

'When was your last period?'

I thought for a minute. 'The end of September.' I had been aware of my lateness, but I had hoped it might just be because of the bombs. I had ignored the sturdiness of my waist and the fact that my breasts were already bursting out of my bras. It had been too much to think about.

'Do you know when the baby was conceived?'

'The fifteenth of October,' I mumbled. 'Exactly then.'

He nodded, his tongue polishing his teeth as he did so. 'Three and a half months. You need to be more careful. You could have lost it. You had a lucky escape.'

I realised that I was only pretending to be relieved, and felt a stab of guilt in a small place above my ribcage where, as a child, I had imagined that my soul lived. I used to draw it into garish portraits of my family, labelling it as an internal organ and adding small penises to the male members of my family because I was intrigued by what I had seen on the small bodies of my little brothers. The teachers at school would cross out my rendering of the spirit, muttering under their breaths that the mystery of the Holy Ghost was not to be labelled, and ignoring the fleshier additions that made Vivien gasp with horror when I showed them to her.

The doctor said that he had better take me home and gripped me uncomfortably under my arm, his thumb digging into my armpit as he helped me to his car. We left by the back door, avoiding the bright eyes and flushed cheeks of the inquisitive dancers. He made me lie across the back seat, like a queen in a carriage. Vivien was at the front door when we got home, her hands on her hips and her eyes wide with fear.

'Please. I'll be alright. I feel fine now.' I tried to escape his grip but his hands were surprisingly tenacious.

'You don't want your mother to know?'

I bit my lip and shook my head. 'She'll be furious. I'm not . . .' I stopped. 'I mean, I . . .' There was nothing I could say. It was obvious that I wasn't married.

He frowned. 'I see. Don't worry. There are lots of girls like you these days. It's this bloody war that does it.' We carried on walking, his head shaking as we approached Vivien. 'No more dancing,' he whispered as he loosened his grip on my elbow. 'You have to look after yourself, in your condition.' He wagged a knobbly finger at me and I could see the silver hairs on the back of his hand bristling with cold. He left me on the doorstep, fluttering like an oversized parcel wrapped untidily in reused brown paper.

His words hung visibly in the crisp February air. They rose smokily and condensed against the window. *Your condition*. I could see that Vivien was turning it over in her mind as if it were an intricate piece of lace, holding it delicately at the sides, reluctant to hold on too tightly. I saw her take in the blood on my dress, and the way my arms were crossed over the lower part of my stomach. I saw her notice the whiteness of my face and the trembling of my knees. Frost began to form on my nose, soaking into my arms and feet.

Suddenly she opened her arms and pulled me towards

her and I felt the warmth of the tops of her arms as they wrapped around me.

'I've got you,' she said, repeating it over and over again until I started to cry with relief. 'I've got you. I've got you.'

'I've been so stupid.' I was choking on my tears.

'Are you okay?' she asked.

I nodded.

'And the baby?'

'It's fine.' I avoided her eye.

She was looking closely at me, stroking my hair. 'Michael?' she asked.

I nodded again.

'Have you told him?'

I began to cry in huge, great, theatrical sobs that caught in my throat and made Vivien bustle me indoors. She laid me on the settee while she went to put the kettle on the stove. She came back in holding a mug of boiling water with a solitary and luxurious mint leaf floating in it. I was crying quietly now. The water turned faintly green.

'What is it? You can tell me. I won't be cross.'

The water spilt onto my knee as I tried to speak, and Vivien jumped over to me, reaching out to steady the mug in my hand. I found the scalding sensation on my knee distracting and strangely comforting.

'He doesn't know. I didn't know until tonight. I knew I was late, but I thought it was because of the bombs.' I took a handkerchief out from the small puffed sleeve of my dress and blew loudly into it. 'I'll write to him tomorrow.'

She nodded gently. 'He'll be back.' She rocked me

gently in her arms. 'And if he doesn't, he'll have me to answer to.'

It makes me smile to think of it now. I was so sure that he would come back to me.

Michael

The doctor said it wasn't a serious stroke. She still thinks it is the cancer that will get me in the end. It was just enough of a stroke to leave me with an ache in my chest and partial paralysis on my left side. I can still write. I can still tap. But I am slipping.

According to my leaflet on the subject, one of the side effects of a lenticulocapsular stroke is the onset of emotional incontinence. Apparently the research suggests that the wide variation in the frequency of cases of emotional incontinence can be comfortably attributed to a lack of methodological heterogeneity, rather than the influence of lesion location. But the symptoms are the same, irrespective of lesion distribution among subjects. Inappropriate and excessive laughter and crying. That is the medical profession's definition of my current status.

It is a strange definition. Surely I am the only one in any position to know if I am being inappropriate and excessive. Surely there must be some background to this evaluation.

I need to tell Anna everything.

.− −. −. .− .− −. −. .− She is so wonderfully nearly symmetrical, even in dits and dahs. Anna. Anna. I mouth the words.

'What is it?' Doreen's chin wobbles as she thuds into my cubicle.

I tap her name again. .– –. –. .–

'Do you need changing?'

I snort with sudden silent laughter. I am shaking in my bed, tears straining at the reddened edges of my eyes. It is exhausting. Doreen rolls me onto my side, her fleshy fingers prodding into my ribcage as she checks my sheets. She grunts and drops me again.

'You're fine,' she announces, and stomps out of the room. 'I'll come back in an hour. We'll sort you out then.'

I giggle at the way she walks with her feet pointing outwards. I find it mildly diverting that her skirt strains at its side stitching, but I am convulsed in uncontrollable spasms of laughter. Am I being excessive, or just inappropriate? There must be a difference.

It is Anna who comes to check my incontinence an hour later. I have just seen a leaf fall from the tree outside my room and I am crying my eyes out. If pressed, I suppose I would concede that this behaviour may be excessive.

I take my pen and tap on the side of my bed.

.– –. –. .– I look at her expectantly.

.... She taps back, and then laughs at my look of surprise. 'My nan taught it to me. That's all she can remember. Hi. And SOS. I was telling her about you.'

I feel a movement in my stomach, a sudden cramp. Anna looks at me in alarm, uncertain whether to fetch Doreen, but I shake my head to make her stay and instead she takes my hand and holds it.

'What is it?' she asks, softly. 'There is something

bothering you. Is it Alf again? Do you want to tell me something else?'

I shake my head. Where do I begin? That has always been the problem. I could say I had simply gone mad from the buzzing of the mosquitoes, or that he did it to himself and I didn't stop him. Or I could pretend that it was because the heat in the hospital tent was getting to me, or the dryness of my throat against my collar distracted me. Or I could try to attribute it to bigger things. The war. Hitler. German rearmament. Versailles. The Archduke. Back and back I could go, making my own actions diminish inside the bowels of the history of the world.

She hands me my notebook and sits in the chair next to my bed and shuts her eyes. 'My shift has finished. I'll wait here.'

We were in the hospital, all of us, dirty and feverish with malaria. I was in the bed next to Brendan. His hair was shining brightly around his head on the white pillow and he was asleep on his front, his bottom too swollen to lie on after the injections. I lay on my side, watching him, unable to close my eyes. The sun was breaking through the cracks in the tent and landing on him in heavy stripes.

Alf was sitting on the floor between us, his legs stretched limply in front of him, poking at a dead cockroach with a stick. He stopped quite suddenly and reached under my bed, pulling out another cockroach, dragging it by the leg. It lay on its back, suffocated into stillness. He lined it up next to the first cockroach. My head was hot and heavy as I watched him crawl around the room, gathering cockroaches, stamping on the living and fussing at the dead. He lined them all up next to my bed.

He looked at me. 'Mick, Mick.' I felt his stick prodding my arm and I tried to lift my head. Tears were pouring down his face. 'What have I done? What would me Mam say? I didn't want to kill them. He said he would shoot me.'

'It's okay,' I told him. 'You had to. If you hadn't killed them, they would have killed us.' My voice was shaky and unpersuasive.

'There was so much blood, Mick. It was so warm.' He was sobbing now, kneeling over the line of cockroaches, almost praying, and it was then that I saw the glint of silver in his hand. Gently, delicately, as if he were icing a cake, he pressed the blade of his knife into the flesh along the top of each shell, and removed the heads of each cockroach, one by one.

'Alf,' I said, nervously.

He looked up at me, but his eyes had glazed over, unable to focus. He stood up abruptly, the knife still in his hand, and leant over Brendan's bed, looking closely at his face.

'Alf.' I said it more firmly this time.

He turned to look at me.

I swung my feet over the side of my bed so that they hung hesitantly over the floor, army issue pyjamas cut off above the ankles, displaying an array of infected mosquito bites. My toenails had turned yellow and there was fluff between my toes.

I felt suddenly incredibly weak from months of quinine dinners and the limited variations of curried goat that we had come up with. My body was raw and sensitive from the constant itching along the seams of my body. I was weak from the sweat that drenched my shirt and made it heavy on my back, and from clinging onto wagons that climbed the thin and windy tracks of the hills of Africa. I was weak from the strain of turning my head away from dead bodies that looked exactly like the one under my pyjamas when it was resting in the sun, and I was tired of the interminable waiting, waiting for it all to end, waiting for messages to come through, waiting for things to happen.

'Alf.'

I could hear him sobbing, breathing too fast, talking under his breath.

I moved slowly towards him, treading around the edges of him. He lifted his head and looked straight through me, his eyes frosted over, tears glinting on his lashes. As he turned away he lifted the knife to Brendan's throat, and I saw Brendan's eyes searching pleadingly for mine, his back rising and falling softly as he lay perfectly still under the blade of the knife.

Let me ask you this, Anna, what would you have done?

I grabbed my rifle from where it was propped up next to my bed and aimed for his left arm. He turned as he heard the click.

I stopped and waited. Brendan made a grab for the knife but Alf turned and lunged for Brendan, the blade pointing at his chest. I pulled the trigger.

I wasn't trying to hurt him. I didn't want to hurt him. I was aiming for his arm. I was just trying to save Brendan.

My knees unlocked with a jolt as the gun fired, and I

fell backwards onto the bed, almost in a swoon. The rifle swung upwards with me, pivoting on my finger so that, as it fired, it no longer pointed at Alf's left arm but hit him squarely in the neck. The knife fell from his hand but Brendan did not move to pick it up. I half-caught Alf as he fell, both of us collapsing under the weight of his body. We lay silently together for a minute, stunned by the finality of it all, his head resting against my stomach, the knife dropped and forgotten. I thought I could feel his lungs moving against my knees.

I manoeuvred my body round and looked at his face. The bullet had gone straight through. Alf's face looked surprised as he rested against me, his left hand lying comfortingly across his chest. I remember the warmth of the blood from his head as it seeped into my pyjamas. And I remember the silence in the ward, broken only by the involuntary chattering of my teeth.

I looked up and noticed a small hole in the canvas roof above Alf's head that had not been there before and I saw the bright white of the sky. And even now, when I see Alf's face in my dreams, as I do every night, there is a bullet-shaped ray of sunlight shining softly on his face.

Is that delusional?

So this is what I need to tell you, Anna, my little girl, that when I was still a boy I killed another boy. He was the same age that you are now, or just about, and he had long arms and a muddy forehead and an accent full of ships and soot, and from that very second until this one right now, my heart turned cold. That is what keeps me awake at night and stops the words in my throat. That is what I have kept to myself all these years, hoping that one day I would forget what I hath wrought.

And now you know.

I look up desperately. *Please don't go. Please don't leave me again.* But I do not say the words.

She is shaking her head as she reads. 'But you didn't mean to do it.' Her hand is on the thinnest part of my arm, gripping it, her eyebrows furrowing as she looks at me. She cannot imagine it, I can see that, and I cannot make her imagine it. I do not want her to imagine it.

'You were only protecting your friend. He was going to kill Brendan.'

I shake my head. I have been over this, again and again. It is not enough. I cling to her hand, bringing it to my lips. I hardly know what I am doing. 'Anna, my Anna.' I growl the words and feel them scrape my decaying throat as they fall out of my mouth into the warm cradle of her palm.

She loosens her grip on my arm and looks at me strangely. She leans towards me, her back as straight as a bootlace and her eyes glistening like secrets. 'Mr Royston, I don't know who you think I am, but I am not your little girl.' She stands up, and places a towel over my forehead. Then, softly this time, she says, 'You should try to get some rest.'

And then she leaves me, just as I knew she would.

Stevie

I fainted in the Churchill Gardens in Bromley last week. I don't remember how it happened. Apparently a girl saw me and called an ambulance and they took me to the hospital. The doctor said it was nothing to worry about. Just a blackout. She was wearing thick brown tights and a dress the colour of pyramids that was too tight about her thighs. I felt she might be missing something important.

The thing is, I told her, I don't remember there being any black. Black would have been an easy, sleepy colour. I remember a lot of red and occasional flashes of blue and white, painted over the black of my eyelids. It made my head ache for days afterwards. It still aches now when I try to remember.

She nodded, and asked if I was a royalist.

I had been feeling dizzy for days before it happened. Names of people I had known for years had started sliding into black holes in my head and it made me nauseous to search for them. Mashing potatoes made me cry, and anything to do with onions put me at risk of complete disintegration. I wondered if it might be the beginnings of dementia.

I had just left the library for a moment to get some

fresh air, and had stumbled a little way down the path towards the bench on the side of the hill from where you can see the railway track and the allotments. The ground was damp and was covered in a sheen of moisture that was slippery underfoot. I could see kids idling on the roundabout and smoking on the slides. I pulled my hood over my head as I walked and I noticed the sharp reflections of the trees in the puddles on the path. I felt the cold seeping into my toes, turning my grey socks dark with the wetness of late autumn. I wrapped my arms around my body and stamped my feet as I walked to keep out the cold.

And suddenly I realised that it was there I had last seen Michael. I remembered it so clearly. We were down by the lake, further down the hill, on the steps of the old stone stage, and Jonathan had come from the opposite direction, limping towards us. I could see a perfect outline of him, but when I tried to look closer I found that the shadows in my memory confused me. My head felt enormous and too heavy and I began to fall backwards until the path crashed into my elbows and there was a pain crushing my chest.

I don't remember anything more after that. That's when it all went blank.

Anna picked me up from the hospital after her shift. I was still slightly dizzy so she took my arm and led me gently to the car door, opening it too wide as if I were a piece of luggage. She folded me neatly at the corners and smoothed out my creases. My insides were wrapped in hospital soup and milk.

'Thank you for coming to get me,' I said.

She looked at me as we pulled into the drive. 'Do you

want to tell me about your fall? Is it because of Granddad?' she asked.

I looked at her and began to cry, because she didn't know what she was asking.

Michael

In the old days, they buried warriors standing up.

We buried Alf on his front in a shallow pit close to the hospital, his head resting on arms. The service was read by a dark-haired priest from the East Midlands. I knelt at the back of a crowd of men, unable to stand for long periods of time because of the shakes that started in my feet and crept up to my neck, and I kept my head down to avoid catching the piercing blue of the priest's eye that sparked as he looked around him. There was no Communion, and I did not have the presumption to approach for a blessing. Three nurses carried me back to my bed as I was shaking so hard that I could barely walk.

Later that day, Brendan and I were informed that our requests for leave had been granted. Brendan was billeted back to Nairobi, and I was to stay with a coffee farmer called Mr Laurence in the Highlands. We shuddered south again in a truck filled with pregnant South African girls in military-style berets being returned home in disgrace from their postings. I sat on the floor of the truck, my head wedged between the door and a girl's knee, avoiding Brendan's eye.

Mr Laurence was waiting for me when we arrived at

Government Road, leaning against a green car with huge wheels and no windows. He had tangled white eyebrows and a Germanic flush in his cheeks, a rather unfortunate feature in the prevailing climate. He looked old and tired, and a little bit embarrassed as he held out his hand to us.

'Which one of you is Michael?' he asked. He had a soft Irish accent and his head wobbled ambivalently as he spoke.

Brendan put his arm around my shoulders and jerked his thumb towards me. We looked at each other for almost a second, and then I dropped my gaze.

'I am,' I said. I slung my bag over my shoulder and shook his hand. 'Pleased to meet you,' I muttered.

'William Laurence, but everyone calls me Laurie.' He ran his fingers through his eyebrows and grinned at me. 'Ready to go?'

I nodded.

'Michael,' Brendan said, grabbing my arm as I walked away. 'Listen to me. It wasn't your fault. You didn't mean to . . .' He stopped and glanced at Laurie, lowering his voice. 'What I mean is, we'll all miss him, especially you, but it wasn't your fault.'

I shook my arm free, and threw my bag into the car, climbing in after it. I felt the backs of my legs sticking uncomfortably to the seat. Brendan was standing over me, watching me. I wanted him to know what to do, like he always had when we were younger, but he just stood there, not saying anything.

Laurie got in next to me. 'It's about an hour's drive from here.' He started the engine, and then looked up at Brendan. 'Is someone coming for you, boy?'

Brendan nodded. 'Yes.' He paused, and then added, 'Look after him for me, will you?'

Laurie nodded, and put the car noisily into gear.

I turned to look out of the window. My head ached where it had been wedged against the door; a soft, dull ache that pressed into my chest and would not go away. We arrived at the house at dusk and followed a muddy track up to the house. Laurie helped me out of the car, holding me steady with his arm. An adolescent donkey was scuffing its hoof apologetically against a rusting metal tank that had turned a golden shade of green, and a dog tilted its head lazily as we passed it on the veranda. I followed Laurie into a large room with rugs on the floor and old armchairs scattered around, and guns propped menacingly in the corners. The window was covered with wire mesh, and a chess set was lying on the floor, abandoned in the middle of a game.

A boy of about fourteen dressed in dark blue pyjamas stood up hastily from one of the armchairs. 'Dinner is served,' he announced, his voice breaking over the ends of his words. 'Outside.'

'This is Peter, my houseboy,' Laurie explained.

I held out my hand and he took it uncertainly. 'Jambo sana,' I attempted, and he smiled shyly at me.

We ate a tender mix of curried goat and chickpeas for dinner, sitting on a rug on the patchy grass next to the fire. I watched Laurie's hands as he ate, noticing the way he brushed every mouthful with his fingers before dabbing it on his tongue, as if he was trying to dust the flavour from it before letting it in.

'This curry is better than I've eaten in months,' I said,

even though I was struggling to eat and could not hold my fork still.

Peter's face cracked into a huge smile and he leant over and shook my hand again. 'I am a wonderful cook,' he announced, 'The best in all of Africa.'

Laurie nodded, and looked faintly amused. 'He is.'

'Well, if you want, maybe I could help you in the kitchen while I'm here?'

Peter's brow crinkled slightly and he glanced at Laurie.

Laurie laughed. 'Peter has very high standards in his kitchen, but I'm sure he can teach you if you want.'

Peter nodded reluctantly, and began to gather the plates. I leant forward to help him but Laurie interrupted me by standing up abruptly and taking my arm to help me stand. 'Not now. Come with me. I want to show you something.'

I followed him slowly back to the house. There was an old bike leaning against the wall, its body tied together with wires that poked out sharply next to the pedals. 'I bought this years ago for my wife when we first came out to Africa.' He looked at me and grinned. 'She was desperate for a bicycle.'

I looked at him and ran my fingers over the saddle. 'Your wife?' I asked.

He smiled. 'Niamh. She died ten years ago.' He coughed. 'Anyway. Climb on.'

He held the bike for me as I lurched unsteadily onto the saddle and leaned into him, unable to balance myself. His strength surprised me. I could feel the solid muscle in his shoulders as he pushed the bike along the path, the metal of the airless wheels grinding under my weight.

He told me about Niamh, about how, during storms,

she loved to sit under her umbrella on the veranda he had built for her, her eyes closed and her head tipped back while the rain drenched her stockings. He told me that his dad had been a carpenter in Cork, the county not the material, and had taught him to build things, how to saw and plane and allow for heat expansion. His dad used to make stools with cleft hooves that clopped against the floor as they wobbled, and chairs with holes in the middle that could be sunk into until your feet no longer touched the floor, and huge carved chests that lay scattered across his workshop floor like frothy ship-wrecks in the gloomy nights of Cork.

Eventually we came to a shed. 'Here we are,' he announced, tipping the bike until my feet touched the ground.

I looked blankly at the small hinges on the side of the shed, and noticed the way it shuffled and squawked.

'Do you know anything about pigeons, boy?'

I shook my head.

'Well, you're going to have to learn. They're the most wonderful creatures in the whole world. Charles Darwin said so, did you know that?'

The birds were lined up in cages on wire shelves, scuffling haughtily around each other. Laurie slid back the bolt of each cage and the small wire doors swung open, releasing a clamour of purple and grey breasts that squeezed past each other and dropped from the ledge. I ducked as the pigeons flew around my head, their wings brushing my neck as they swooped upwards in a terrifying flap of noise that felt as if it might be coming from the inside of my head.

When the air was quiet again, I saw that there was

still one bird left in the cage, a fat white pigeon with pink wings.

'Come on,' Laurie said softly to the bird, coaxing it towards him. When it was close enough, Laurie reached inside the cage and clamped his hands around the middle of the pigeon. He brought it out gently and handed it to me. 'Meet Mr Redmond,' he said. 'He's a cautious one, this one. They all were, the parliamentarians.'

I took Mr Redmond in my hands and felt his soft bones sinking into his fleshy body. I began to feel nauseous. His muscles twitched so I loosened my grip and felt his wings pushing against my hands.

'Let him go, my boy. Throw him up,' Laurie said softly, gesturing upwards with his hands.

I lifted my trembling hands above my head and opened my fingers. Mr Redmond pushed against my palms with his sharp feet, and the tips of his wings brushed my wrists. He flapped harder, rising away from me, and I looked at Laurie and began to laugh.

We went to the pigeon loft every morning that week. The sky would still be grey when we left the house, with shades of yellow sunlight beginning to drip into the eastern horizon. I would follow Laurie blearily along the path that bordered the coffee fields until we reached the shed, and then I would sit on the roof of the loft while the birds flew around us, until Laurie called them back by shaking his tin of dried grain.

Gradually I learnt all the names of the pigeons, each of them being named after a great Irish Republican, and I learnt how to tell one from another. I learnt that Eoin MacNeill had a bluer neck than Padraig Pearse, and that

Eamon de Valera had one webbed foot. I knew which ones would return first and which ones would return reluctantly, landing petulantly on the roof of the loft hours later and stamping their feet crossly until Laurie came back in the afternoon to feed them and let them in, while I ground spices for Peter in the kitchen. I learnt how to hold the pigeons and when to throw them. I listened to Laurie's soft voice as he told me where each of them had come from, and their role in the fight for the independence of Ireland.

He waited for me to say something back, to tell him why I did not sleep at night and why I shook uncontrollably for hours at a time, but the words would not come. He asked if I had any letters to send home when Peter next went into the town and he did not blink when I told him that I could not write, not now. He did not ever probe, but instead he gave me the more docile of his pigeons to hold, and their soft bodies would warm my arms as I held them tightly against my chest before lifting them above my head and opening my fingers.

After six days with Laurie and Peter, I had to report back to the Army HQ in Nairobi. My shakes returned so that by the time I had bumped my way to Nairobi in Laurie's car I could hardly stand up. Brendan was waiting in the office in a small wooden chair when I arrived, his pockets bulging with embezzled supplies of quinine. He grinned nervously at me when I came in, and we patted each other timorously on the back.

'Michael.' He took my arm tightly, and swung me round so that I was facing him. 'What I meant to say the other day was . . .' He paused. 'I didn't ever thank you for the other night. I know you did what you did to save me.'

I looked at him. 'But I couldn't hold the gun. I didn't mean to kill him. I didn't . . .' The words stuck in my throat.

'I know,' he said. 'I know you didn't mean to kill him. The gun fell. But these things happen in wars. It's not real life out here. You have to forget it.'

I smiled uncertainly at him. We were interrupted by a huge-shouldered medical officer from South Africa, who poked his head into the room and called me in for my inspection.

I lay down on a low bed in the medical room and the doctor leant over me while my body continued to shake. He tapped my knee brusquely with a burnished silver pen and nothing happened. He shook the pen and turned it upside down, as if it were the pen that was deficient, and I told him that I thought I had malaria. He nodded absently and inserted a thermometer into my mouth. My teeth jabbered violently against the glass. He held my leg aloft and began tapping the sole of my foot with his fingernail while my leg shuddered in his hands. I thought I might be about to die. He kneaded my foot with his huge thumb and I flinched.

'As I thought.' He replaced my leg on the bed and bent down to retrieve a yellow piece of paper from his bag. 'Yis, yis. No more heroics for you,' he said, handing me the yellow paper. 'You can thank your lucky stars for those. That Rommel character isn't going to get you.' He rapped my big toe smartly with his clipboard and threw my shirt back to me. 'I'll tell them you're to stay here until you're well enough to travel.' He slotted the pen behind his ear and slipped his thermometer into his jacket pocket, and then he sidestepped gracefully between the thin curtains of the surgery.

I looked at the paper as it trembled in my hand. I saw that he had written *FLAT FEET* in the box marked *Reason for Discharge*. So that was that. It was over.

Brendan was dispatched in a truck to the RAF head-quarters in Cairo where he would be training men in high-speed telegraphy as the front line approached. I waved him off from the hospital gates. The sky turned pink as his red hair receded on the horizon, his hand held aloft as he balanced on the tips of his beautifully arched feet. I never saw him again.

Stevie

I had been dreading Emily's birth. I found the very thought of it terrifying. I didn't see how, on a purely mechanical basis, it would be physically possible.

My baby girl decided to enter the world on the same day that the Germans arrived at the Eastern Front. I had not heard from Michael for five months and the news was filled with reports of rivers of blood, of Russian peasants leaving their homes and burning the countryside behind them. It felt like a bad omen.

A midwife called Josephine came to the house to deliver her as there was a shortage of beds at the hospital. She was hot and plump, and dressed in a brown uniform with a small brown hat. She made me lie on a sheet on Vivien's bed, barely able to breathe, while she defrocked me and prodded me and checked my dilations. She called Vivien onto the landing and whispered to her, and then they both bundled me into Josephine's car to go to Guy's Hospital. Vivien grabbed my hand as I struggled to my feet, my weight supported by Josephine's superior bulk, and forced her wedding ring onto my swollen finger.

There were complicated complications with the birth that were never properly explained to me. Vivien appeared at the hospital and was clutching at my arm when Emily's foot finally wiggled its toes in the open air and she was dragged out, upside down and bright blue, onto the starched hospital bed. I remember wishing that blood could be a more neutral colour, more white-washed. It was an exhausting shade of red. It made my eyes tired just looking at it and it attracted too much attention. I heard a baby's cry and felt a rush of blood leaving my body, and then I passed out.

When I woke up, I could not lift my head. Josephine was bundling a pile of towels drenched in blood into a white bag.

'Is it . . . ?' I asked weakly.

'Oh, you're awake,' Josephine said abruptly. 'Hold on, I'll go and get her.' She returned with my baby and laid her gently in my arms. 'There,' she said, more softly this time. She kissed the baby on the top of her oversized head, and then reached over and placed her hot, chubby palm on my forehead. It smelt of hospital soap and old towels. For a second I thought she was going to kiss me too, but instead she leant gently towards me and whispered, 'She's beautiful.'

I smiled feebly. 'She is.'

Josephine hesitated. 'How do you feel?'

I tried to nod. The effort clouded my eyes and I thought I might faint. 'Fine,' I said eventually.

Josephine returned her hand to my head, holding me still. 'I'm afraid the doctor has been called away so you can't talk to him directly but you have lost a lot of blood. There were a lot of stitches.'

'Is she ill?' I asked, tightening my hold around Emily.

'Your baby is absolutely fine.' She brushed a piece of

hair from my eye and I resisted the urge to lean my head into her huge aproned bosom. Josephine stood up to leave but turned back to me at the door. 'I'll send your mother in.' She adjusted her small brown hat. 'She's waiting outside.'

I nodded and held my baby girl tightly against my chest as the door closed behind Josephine, and I thought of Michael's arms in the Peckham Lido, holding us.

Michael

'Michael. Michael. Michael.' There is no variation in tone, no urgency. The voice pauses, and then starts again.

I try to open my eyes, the muscles in my eyelids straining as I pull them apart. The doctor is bending over me, watching me. She looks tired. Doreen is standing behind her, wringing the curtain between her pudgy fingers. It is cold in here. Why is it so cold? I can't stop shaking.

I have had this before, you see. I know what happens. There is only one cure, and I can't imagine that it has made it onto the syllabus at medical school. It wouldn't be very professional.

Don't get me wrong, there was nothing unprofessional about the treatment I received in Africa. Tabitha had that subtlety of approach that defines any true professional, eliminating any requirement to delve into the practicalities of the matter at hand. There was no discussion of any of the messier details. There were small courtesies that served to smooth over the awkward patches. There was regulation, efficiency, certainty. These were added extras, certainly, but you get what you pay for. I have

151

always thought that there is much to be admired in the professional.

There were others, before Tabitha, who came into the army barracks in Nairobi where I was waiting to be well enough to travel and who offered the same sort of service. They came in with swinging ears and plumped-up bottoms, winking and hooting. Most of them couldn't have been more than fourteen years old. They were loud and frothy, with hair cropped close to their heads, but their eyes were glassy and bored as they looked around them. They whispered between themselves as they walked, and occasionally you could see their shoulder blades shudder gently as they left the gates of the army camp. *Was it me,* you are left to wonder, *that inspired that shudder? Do I disgust you that much?* Do you see what I mean? Most unprofessional.

The first time I saw Tabitha, she was trying to thread a shoelace through a thin hole in the sole of her sandal at the door of the hospital tent. I called out from my bed to ask her if she wanted to borrow my knife. She stared at me, then threw her head back until it cracked on her neck and laughed. She had a crowded mouth of uneven teeth and a violently pink tongue and was missing the lower half of one ear. The other ear hung down her neck in a distended loop, and her hair fell in detachable ringlets.

'Where you learn to speak Swahili like some Quakerboy?' she asked, a fresh peal of laughter breaking from her lips with each step she took towards me. She burrowed the blade of my knife into the thin sole of her sandal and pushed the lace through, still snorting softly to herself.

'You got the shakes?' she asked, as she handed the knife back to me.

I nodded.

'Hmph. I know something that sort that out. Better than any doctorman.' She pulled the lace through the sole, grimacing in satisfaction. She sat on the edge of my bed and tied the laces in bows on the tops of her feet. Her back was smooth as she leant forwards, concentrating. She stood up and the sandals dragged snappily across the floor as she walked. She saw me watching her and came back over to my bed.

'What you do is this,' she whispered, her distended ear swinging over me as she leaned a little closer. 'You come to Eastleigh and you ask for Tabitha. Ask a Taximan and they find me. Tell them shaky Quakerboy looking for Tabitha.'

I nodded. Her bossiness was oddly comforting.

'And bring some broken clothes needing mending. I don't want the neighbours thinking I am common street-walker woman,' she added, frowning crossly at me. 'I am mender woman. That is all.'

I watched the curtains fall behind her. Her footsteps stopped outside. 'I free on Tuesdays,' I heard her say, and then she shuffled off. I shut my eyes and tried to sleep.

I found Tabitha easily the next Tuesday, my bag of snipped seams slung over my shoulder. A small boy in shiny blue shorts came to the door of the hut and stared at me under his long eyelashes. He was sucking a piece of sugar cane. Tabitha came to the door, clipping a ringlet to the back of her head.

'I knew it be you,' she said, pushing the boy outside

and talking quickly to him in a language I could not understand. She took the bag from my shoulder. 'We talk price later.' The boy watched me as I followed her inside.

Tabitha was nothing like Stevie. She had dark liquid eyes and smelt of sour dough. She squatted in front of me and I felt her hands kneading my body as she undid the buttons of my trousers. My body ached where she touched it.

I went to her with my same bag of broken clothes every Tuesday. I brought roasted meat and eggs for her, and biscuits for the boy. I would take off my shoes and follow her through to the inner room of the hut with its discoloured pile of woven mats. She would unbutton my shirt and slide my trousers down, and I would avert my eyes from the sucked pieces of sugar cane that lurked resentfully in shadowy corners.

I watched as she stepped out of her clothes. She had low-hanging breasts that she brushed over my face and huge nipples that were deliciously bumpy. She moved across me in circles and, for a tiny moment every Tuesday, I would feel my rubbery heart contract and my lungs prickle and stretch.

Afterwards I would unravel onto the mat, no longer able to hold back the waves of tiredness that over-whelmed me, and I would fall deeply asleep, my mouth open and my hands clasped over my stomach.

Those were the only times I ever slept during those months. It was an empty, satisfying sleep. Tabitha would wake me at dusk and we would eat the food that I had brought and talk politely about the weather. This is the sort of thing I mean about her professionalism. She was

154

so professional that I began to tell her things about myself. I began to believe that when she laughed she was not thinking of the money that I had put in the small cloth bag she kept on a string around her neck, or of the roast chicken on the table. I told her that I had had a friend called Alf who had died and she stopped eating and listened, and held my hand under the table. I didn't tell her that I killed him. I told her about my father and about Brendan and about how to make a crystal diode radio. She thought that was a great joke. She asked me politely as she buttered her bread if I had a wife back home, and I almost told her about Stevie but the words wouldn't come.

And eventually, after I had been visiting for nearly two months, she began to tell me about her own life. She told me that her family had been squatters on a white farm in the Highlands of Kenya but that she had been sent to the Quaker Mission when she was nine. A pink man from Scotland with red ears and curly black hair had sung to them in a high voice for several hours each day. He taught them to read from the Bible and to write using sticks in the sand. He told them that God was a light, and that each of them carried a light inside themselves and that this light was God. The children at the Mission had looked at each other and wondered.

When Tabitha left the Mission three years later and went back to her parents' hut, she knew all about the light inside her. Her dad was less convinced. He confiscated all the money she earned and beat her if she complained. When he found the coins she had buried in the ground underneath her sleeping mat he cut off the bottom of her left ear, so she left for Nairobi with one and a half ears and a grandiose English vocabulary.

She furrowed her forehead. 'I still have my light, but now also I am a Muslim. You see,' she said, leaning gravely in towards me, 'it is unclear, the law on Quaker women. Muslim women can own huts by themselves. So perhaps it is best to be both.'

I nodded in emphatic agreement.

She told me later that business was good because of the Italian prisoners who brought sheets with their POW numbers emblazoned across the corners. They brought pocketfuls of thick, government-supplied condoms that she kept in a tin in the corner of the room, and of which I availed myself when the occasion arose. She told me that she liked me because I paid white prices and I spent the whole day sleeping but she could still charge me for a full day.

I was flattered by these small confidences. I wanted to know about the little boy with the shiny blue shorts and the sugar cane habit but she swerved gracefully around him and I knocked my knees against the solid boundaries of the life she would allow me to see.

She was right about her therapy. I stopped shaking for longer and longer after each session, hours turning into days, until finally I had stopped altogether. The army doctor came to see me and patted his breast pocket with his silver pen and looked proudly at his notebook. He told me that I was well enough to travel, and that he would personally see to it that I was on the next passage home. I looked at him in horror as I realised that I was expected to return to England and take up some sort of wartime employment as though nothing had happened.

I imagined trying to explain all this. I imagined my mum smiling incomprehensibly as she ran wet shirts through the mangle in the backyard. I imagined my father looking up from his tax returns and nodding when he saw me. And then I thought of Stevie and felt a deep rush of shame that dug into my stomach and burned the back of my neck. I could not go back to England.

I decided to run away.

Doreen is holding my arm while the doctor brandishes the needle.

'This will stop those shakes for a bit,' the doctor tells me. 'Hold still, Doreen.' She turns back to me, 'Now, Michael, this won't hurt, but there's going to be a faint pricking sensation.'

Perhaps she is not so innocent after all. I giggle incontinently and feel Doreen's grip loosening on my arm.

Stevie

I remember how, between the flash of an exploding bomb and the sound of it shuddering under your feet and up your spine until it bursts out of your ears, there was always a moment of absolute, illuminated silence. And it was there, in that tiny moment of anticipation and uncertainty, that I still believed Michael was not dead.

I had not heard from him for nearly six months when a letter finally arrived from Africa. His last postcard had said that no letters from home were getting through to him, so Vivien thought that it was bound to work both ways. Africa was not exactly Belgium, she argued with indisputable reason. It was so far away and the ships were probably all being sunk. It stood to reason that there would be no word from Michael until there were bananas in the greengrocers again.

Michael's mother was not fully convinced of the link between her son and bananas. She wore her rosary beads around her wrist in the shelter just in case. Praying for his soul, she explained to the woman next to her. She knitted cardigans and shawls for Emily and came to visit once a week, telling me not to mind her husband who refused to acknowledge Emily's existence. He would come round, she said, when Michael was back. She told me that her husband still spent his nights in Benedict's old bed, his hands clasped and his nose whistling while the bombs fell.

'He'll be back, love,' she would say, balancing her cup of tea on her lap, and we would nod unconvincingly to each other, neither of us wishing to be the first to stop.

It was only during the flash, for that magical second, that I *knew* he was alive and would be coming back.

In the months leading up to Emily's birth and for several weeks after her arrival, we spent most of our nights in the public shelter just off the Old Kent Road. It was a dimly lit labyrinth, filled with small boys swapping pieces of their shrapnel collections, and rowdy girls imitating Shirley Temple in *The Little Princess*. The women sang ''Enery the Eighth, I yam, I yam' and 'Roll out the Barrel', and Vivien would smile tightly, surreptitiously admonishing me if I forgot myself and began to sing along. She would elbow her way through the crowds, my younger brothers clinging to the utility boiler suit that she had constructed for such occasions, until she found Colin.

Colin was Vivien's lucky mascot. He had the whitest teeth I had ever seen and an old Trinidadian accent that neither Vivien nor I could fully understand. He gave my brothers matchsticks to chew, the sort of gift which, under normal circumstances, would have provoked spasms in my mum's arms, but coming from Colin, Vivien hardly even twitched. We would settle down on the bench next to Colin and pass Emily between us, watching him through half-closed eyes as he checked on the sleeping crowds, the bright white of his ARP tin hat contrasting

159

sharply with the darkness of his skin. Vivien thought he was the best thing since sliced bread.

'If it weren't for that nice Colin, we'd all be dead,' Vivien would pronounce when we pleaded with her to let us stay at home during the raid and go under the stairs like everyone else we knew. 'One day you'll thank me for this. And I hope you'll thank Colin too.'

On the day that Michael's letter came, the siren went off as I was on my way home from the Ministry on the bus. I went straight to the shelter, and found Vivien already there, dismissively holding the sleeve of Colin's coat whilst talking to the lady next to her. Colin smiled at me, making no attempt to retrieve his arm, and handed me a matchstick.

'Stevie! There you are!' Vivien said, breathlessly pushing her neighbour aside so that I could sit down. 'There's a letter.' She dragged a crumpled envelope from her pocket and thrust it at me. Emily began to cry.

We both ignored her. The letter was cold in my hand and too thin, its seal frosted shut. This was not what I had imagined.

'Wait,' Vivien said. 'Here.' She grabbed my hand and dragged it across her so that I fell onto Colin's arm, making him jump slightly.

'Mum! What are you doing?'

'Shhhh,' she whispered conspiratorially. 'For luck.' Colin grinned at me and shrugged his shoulders, accustomed as he was by now to Vivien's superstitions. She let go of my hand and I removed it apologetically from Colin's arm. 'There, now you can read it.'

I unfolded the thin piece of paper and read what Michael had written, and as I read I saw the flash that

I had been praying against illuminating the space in front of my eyes. I wriggled my toes uncomfortably inside my slightly battered, too-big boots, trying not to cry. I stood up, and then sat down again. Vivien held my arm. Colin reached over to touch my shoulder and Vivien flapped him away.

'What is it? What does he say?' she asked.

I shook my head and stood up, walking out of the shelter and onto the street, the tears burning the sides of my eyes. My boots felt as if they were full of tiny stones, and the sharpness of them made me flinch with each step.

Why did he have to tell me her name? Tabitha. She sounds like a cat.

Tabeethaaaa.

He didn't even mention Emily. Even then, with his letter in my hand and the light shining on my face, I still did not fully believe it. I stood in the street and put my hands over my ears so that I would not hear the bang.

Michael

After Alf died, I found it impossible to write. My post-cards lay blank and crumpled in my pocket. It didn't help that we had not received any news from home for months. We wrote into a vacuum for the whole of that year. Our letters were lost in the desert in 1941, stock-piled in Cairo, or sunk at sea without even reaching Africa. Arranging for the distribution of letters was the first thing Monty did, I heard later, when he took charge in 1942, but by then I had been discharged, leaving no address.

The night before I left the hospital in Nairobi, I wrote a letter to Stevie. My fingerprints smudged the paper as I spread it shakily in front of me. The pen was grimy where I held it. The tangled hairs on my arms bristled with dirt that would not come out. When I rubbed my legs over the bucket in the washroom it felt like I was soaping down an elephant. I remembered the powdery whiteness of Stevie's skin as she lay underneath me on Peckham Rye, soft and perfect and smelling of chopped cabbages, and I knew that I did not want her to under-stand this dirt.

I spent hours composing the letter. I rolled the pen in my hand, biting its end and drawing on my arm as I considered what to write. I tried to describe what it was like, to explain what I had done. I told her about the rain and the Italians. I told her about the beetles, how they were all in a line. I told her about Brendan's eyes and that I had been aiming for Alf's arm.

I wrote and wrote, and when I had finished I put down my pen and lit a cigarette. The letter lay on the table in front of me. I held the cigarette between my finger and thumb, the same finger and thumb I had left England with two years before, and which now felt damaged. As I read over what I had written I was aware of the smoke leaving my body, thinning out as it rose further from its source, scattering, until it could hardly be distinguished from the normal, non-tobacco air. And I realised that she would forgive me.

I stubbed out my cigarette and tore up the letter. I knew that something had happened which should change everything. It should not be possible for a boy to be killed and for everything to remain as it was before. People have to care about other people. Things should not just fade into other things until they are indistinguishable. There must be some responsibility.

I took a new piece of paper and addressed it once more to Stevie. I wrote three simple lines, signed my name, and then folded the piece of paper into quarters, sharpening its edges as I slid it into the envelope. In the letter I sent, I did not include any mitigating factors. I did not mention Alf, or Brendan, or the Italians. I did not tell her about the malaria ward, or Addis Ababa, or Laurie's pigeons. I told her only one thing. I gave her small details. The blue shorts. The woven mats. I didn't offer any excuses or reasons. I wanted no understanding from her. She must feel no guilt. She must rip up the letter and stamp it into the ground, rubbing it until the paper splits and the words fall off onto the pavement. And then she must forget all about me.

That would be my punishment.

I hid my love for her in the gaps between the few, simple lines of the letter; heavy, obvious lines that she might never think to look between. I held a tissue under my eyes as I wrote to prevent any drops from spoiling the effect.

I remember how the lady at the Post Office counter laid the envelope on the silver scale next to her till. It was one of those thin, blue envelopes with red darts around the side. I put the coins on the counter. She took them and threw the letter into the box behind her. I watched it land carelessly on top of the scrawling pile of letters, unretractable. She looked up at me again.

'Anything else?'

I hesitated. 'No, that's all. Thank you.' I opened the door.

The red dust of the road leapt into the pores of my cheeks as I left the shop to return to the barracks. I noticed how everybody looked at me as I passed. They looked at my uniform, and they saw what I had done. They saw Alf's face staring upwards, and they saw his blood on my skin. I felt my shirt clinging hotly to my skin, reminding me of the weight of his arm as it lay limply across me. I lowered my eyes and kept on walking.

Stevie

I didn't hear the bang straight away. I had a stubborn Bolshevik streak that made me shut my ears to it. I fought against it. I barricaded myself in. I slashed and burned as I retreated, leaving nothing in my wake. I would not budge. It was Michael I was waiting for. I tore his letter into tiny pieces and refused to believe it. I was convinced that there had been some mistake. He hadn't even mentioned Emily.

And as for Tabitha, well, that wasn't even a real name.

Indeed, throughout the weeks that the Germans were busily breaking through the Eastern Front and marching towards Moscow, and just as the first pale strands of hair were pushing through the soft skin of Emily's scalp, Josef Stalin and I, in our separate beds, folded our arms in disbelief at our respective betrayals, and refused to believe the extent of what we were being told.

Vivien's eyebrows adopted an expression of permanent outrage, and she became decidedly offish with Colin. Even when my sister Mary arrived home, delightedly waving a single ill-gotten toilet roll, Vivien barely showed so much as a single tooth of a smile. The air raids became less and less frequent, with more and more German troops being poured into the deep hole that was the Eastern Front.

Josef came round a little quicker than I did. He ordered his troops to form mass barricades after receiving enough reports to convince him that the Red Army were being slaughtered in their thousands. As for me, I waited for two whole weeks before surreptitiously checking the Ministry of Labour files in the Newington Butts office. I found two Tabithas registered in the catchment area at the Camberwell end of Denmark Hill, and realised that perhaps it was a real name.

In which case, perhaps it was true.

And that was when I heard the bang, and realised that he was not coming back.

Michael

I arrived back at Laurie's farm at dusk the following day, uninvited and unannounced. The post-malarial ache in my head was dripping slowly down towards the middle of my chest. I didn't go straight up to the house but instead took the crumbling path that ran alongside the edge of the coffee fields. The coffee leaves were richly and fatly green after a month of relentless downpours, and the path was tangled beneath my feet. The air smelt of frangipani. I took large flattening steps, suddenly impatient to be found. Pigeons straggled in the sky, following the rhythmic rattle of grain in a tin.

I followed the noise until I saw Laurie's cobwebby hair glistening in the soft light of the suspended lamp. Laurie looked up at me without surprise and raised his finger to his lips. I watched as he inspected each returning bird, running his eyes over their oily wings and speckled flanks, offering grain hidden in the deep lines of his hand.

He looked at me. 'Do you want to take the next one?'

I nodded and cupped my hand to receive the grain. The next exhausted bird arrived, and I stretched out my arm, and Michael Collins was thus invited to peck at the palm of my hand while Laurie noted down his time and safe arrival.

'If you're planning on staying,' he said softly, not looking up at me, 'you'd better start by giving that cage on the end a quick scrape. I didn't have time to do it today. It's mating season. They go crazy in mating season.'

I grinned and unhooked the spatula from the hook on the wall and began to scrape, and that was when it was arranged that I would stay.

When the last bird had arrived, we locked the door of the loft and I took the lamp from the beam above the doorway. Peter startled me by appearing quite suddenly out of the darkness, three sharpened sticks in his belt and a bow slung across his shoulder. He nodded when he saw me.

'Peter,' I said, holding my hand out to him. 'Any lions out tonight?'

He took my hand, his head nodding excitedly. 'Not tonight. It is quiet tonight. Welcome back, *bwana*.'

We walked in silence to the house, listening for rustles. The smell of masala and cardamom wafted in the air. I had forgotten how loud the night could be on the farm.

The next morning, Laurie gestured towards the bathtub outside the window and told me to take my clothes off. 'Peter's finally got that bloody ass moving,' he said.

I went to the door and saw the donkey struggling up the side of the garden, sloshing water from the green oilcans that were strapped to its sides. Peter was lazily flicking a whip over the donkey's hind legs, hardly seeming to touch him at all. It took three trips for the donkey to fill the bath for me. I folded my clothes neatly in a pile on the soil next to me and climbed in, resting my neck against the rusty edges of the bath as I lay in the cool water. The trees were noisy with invisible animals. I wafted the water against the side of the bath with my hands and watched the ripples bouncing into each other. I submerged my head and lifted my feet out of the other end of the tub and lay perfectly still.

Suddenly I felt something land on my stomach. It was small and heavy. I grabbed it and felt it moving in my hand, slimy and muscular. I pictured a fleshy, beating heart. I leapt up and fell out of the bath. I was screaming and embarrassingly naked. Peter and Laurie came running to find me. 'A heart!' I shouted. 'A heart landed on me.'

Peter dived his arm into the bathtub and pulled out a dark green frog. He cupped it in his hand and made me look at it so that I could see its eyes. And then he began to laugh. I crossed my arms defensively over my body and felt my breath begin to come again.

'I'm sorry,' I gasped. 'I thought . . .' I stopped, suddenly ashamed of my outburst.

Peter put the frog back in the bath. 'He always comes to visit when people take bath. He likes bath. Don't worry. You will get used to him.' He handed me the towel that he had laid out for me. 'Dry with this. And then run. You will feel better when you run.'

So I did. I dried my face and left the rest of my body to dry in the sun and I ran. I ran with no shoes, ignoring the army instructions to wear boots at all times, ignoring the snakes that slithered away from me as they heard me coming, ignoring the sharp stones and the broken branches that cut into my skin. I ran and ran and when I got back I was so tired that I had to lie down on the grass to stop the exhaustion from overwhelming me.

My pigeon education began in earnest the next day. Laurie taught me about squibs and squeakers, yearlings and eye cere. He taught me the differences between logans and gurneys. I learnt to tell a cock from a hen, and an inbred specimen from a crossbred. I scrawled notes detailing the intricacies of apple bodies, bent keels, roomy hens and fret marks. I looked out for telltale signs of red mites and feather lice. I kept records of the times of each pigeon in black receipt books with yellow pages, and I bruised my knuckles scraping dried shit out of the loft at dusk as we waited for our pigeons to return.

We were training the pigeons to be athletes. Three mornings a week I would strap a cage of Irish republicans to the back of Laurie's skeletal bicycle and wobble jauntily into Nairobi. My buttocks ached permanently from these journeys. There was a network of bus drivers, station porters, old safari guides and army men who colluded in the implementation of our rigorous training plan. They would fling the crates of squawking pigeons into luggage compartments, and take the instructions of liberation, crumpling them irreverently into their pockets. We would agree the locations and times at which they were to release the pigeons, and I would hand over bribes, pocketfuls of potatoes or small bags of coffee.

They all had their price. Kilimo, a local bus driver on the Eldoret road, requested nothing more for his trouble than a game of poker with me. We would crouch over the crate of pigeons, our thighs sticking to the disembodied car seats appropriated by the chai stall at the bus station, and we would play cards. The crowds would gather, drawn in by the soft flicker of cards against thumbs. The men behind us would point out runs and flushes, openly discussing our hands. They would overturn the top card of the dealer's pile and announce its salient features. Children would share out the discarded cards, bending them at the edges and fraying their corners. The bus would start to rock and squawk as its passengers grew hot and impatient. Kilimo would gasp with delight when I laid down a good hand, and the crowd would erupt with excitement. I found it difficult to reciprocate in the same measure, not through a misplaced sense of competitiveness, but through sheer embarrassment. When it was over, Kilimo would depart in a flurry of horns and hands slapping the side of the bus, taking the crate of pigeons with him to release when he arrived in Eldoret.

The station porter, Silas, was also a crucial figure in our operations. He was a huge man with large eyes and a wrist that glittered with women's bracelets, and a voice so deep that when he spoke I felt my insides slipping out of me. He was in charge of coordinating the conductors to take the birds on the train, and then collecting the crates that arrived back at the station weeks later. Silas kept a Bible in the janitor's cupboard, on the shelf next to the spare tin of blue paint. He would place it on the table between us and he would ask that I listen to him reading, always the same passage from the Song of Solomon, and I had to correct his pronunciation. He would tap his foot as he read, swaying softly, and then would disapprovingly accept the mealies that I drew from my pockets to give to the train drivers. I would take the returned pigeon crates from under his desk and balance them on the back of my bike as I cycled home, stopping at the market to buy whole carrots bent into tins and slabs of dark chocolate to eat while we waited for the pigeons to arrive home.

I went to sleep dreaming of pigeons. I read books about pigeons. I considered new ways of training pigeons for night-flying as I sifted absently through trays of drying coffee beans. I developed experiments to test the vision of my favourite pigeons, the ones for which I had grand plans of gold medals and Victoria Crosses. I recorded their times and their moods. I invented new lightweight non-metal identification rings to attach to the legs of my champion pigeons. Laurie was delighted at my interest.

I tore articles from newspapers and put them into small tubes that I attached to the legs of the birds before a flight, so that I could test the efficacy of the message-holders in the rain. I would line the bedraggled notes brought back by the pigeons along my windowsill so that they would be dry for the next training session, and sometimes during the night they would flutter onto the floor next to my bed, so that in the morning I would wake up and see a floor covered with scraps of paper that looked like a torn-up letter.

And so, in the end, even the pigeons conspired to remind me of Stevie. I would be dreaming of pigeons and then suddenly, instead of a ripped-out newspaper article, I would picture the letter I had written to her dangling from the leg of a pigeon. I would imagine a red-faced and panting pigeon crashing onto the pave-ment in front of her, splattering its feathers onto her shoes. I would imagine her taking the letter from the leg of the pigeon and turning it over. And I would imagine her eyes turning blue and her dimples digging into her cheeks when she saw that it was from me.

I polished this image of her and left it there, because I did not want to imagine what would come after she opened the letter.

Stevie

I met Jonathan at the door of the Ministry office with newspaper print smudged under his eyes in careless fingerprints. He was sitting on the top step, waiting for the door to be unlocked. He had dark hair and seaweed eyes, and he was using a magnifying glass to read the newspaper even though he was not much older than me. He wore heavy boots that were laced up at the front and showed a pair of green socks over the top of them.

I was early for my shift. Strands of hair had escaped from their clips during my journey across London, and were falling over the stiff neck of my blouse. He watched me as I tidied my hair, securing it with brown grips, and then smoothing down my skirt. I unlocked the door and he stood up to follow me.

I turned around. 'Do you have an appointment?' I asked.

He nodded, his suit high-shouldered and tight across his chest. 'I'm a bit early. I have a meeting with the manager.' He put the magnifying glass in his pocket. 'I've lost my glasses,' he explained, seeing the look on my face. 'It hurts my eyes.'

'Do you want to come in and wait?' I asked, turning the key in the lock and pushing the door open.

He nodded and rubbed his left eye, extending the dark smudge onto his cheek. I stepped forward to go into the office but then stopped and turned around. He was waiting on the step below me, so that his head was level with mine. I reached impulsively into my handbag and brought out a handkerchief. I wrapped it around my finger, and had to stop myself from licking the end of it. Emily hated it when I did this. She hated the way I delved into her ears and wiped the corners of her eyes every morning with my screwed-up handkerchief. Even Vivien thought I was too thorough, that I should leave a thin layer of wax in Emily's ears and allow a delicate film to gather across her eyes. She considered mucus to be a sort of natural defence, a filter for the senses. She said I was making Emily needlessly vulnerable.

'May I?' I asked.

He nodded, his expression slightly confused.

I raised the handkerchief to his face and dabbed it against the fingerprints. 'It's newspaper print,' I said.

He shut his eyes and when I had finished, he looked back at me and reached out his hand, and then he touched the top of my right cheek with his fingers as if there was something there that he wanted to rub away too.

'What is it?' I asked, folding the handkerchief back into my pocket, and thinking of stray hairs, of tears. I looked away.

'I don't know,' he said. 'But there is something, isn't there?'

I wondered when I had become so transparent. He grinned and let his hand fall, brushing my cheek as he did so, and it was then that I first noticed his smell. It was a curious thing, that smell. It was not unpleasant

175

or what you might call odorous. Just a lived-in, salty smell I had never smelt before. We stood together on the step and I opened my lungs and breathed him in.

He put his hand back in his pocket. I blinked nervously as I looked at him, and then felt suddenly embarrassed in case I had winked by mistake. I turned and pushed open the door so that he would not see my neck reddening. He sat on a wooden chair in the corridor outside my office, and I could hear his feet shuffling as I removed a small pile of blank forms from the drawer in my desk and arranged them neatly in front of me.

Eva trotted in, five minutes late and humming, and she came over to sit on the edge of my desk.

'Where were you last night then?' I asked, hastily moving my pile of papers as she swung her legs up onto the table.

She laughed and put her finger to her lips, feigning shyness. 'Clapham,' she admitted finally, looking at me out of the corner of her eye. 'You should come next time.'

I smiled and shook my head, as I always did when she asked me to accompany on her nocturnal jaunts.

She looked disappointed for a moment, distracted, but then she smiled brightly and lifted her leg, instructing me to feel how soft her stockings were. I rubbed them with the back of my hand and made appreciative noises while she adjusted her shoes and aligned the seam. She took out a small tortoiseshell comb and fixed it in her hair. I got up and went to the door, pretending that I was going to see if anybody was queuing to register with us. But really, I wanted to see if he was still there. I could see his boots, waiting, beneath his too-short suit trousers. I smiled and felt for the handkerchief in my handbag.

The smell of him lingered between the cracks of my palm until lunchtime. The wind blew my hair into my mouth and around my eyes as I walked to Kennington Park to eat my sandwiches, but I hardly noticed. I did not reach up to correct it but instead let it fall around my face and down my neck.

He was talking to Eva in our office when I got back. He stood up, embarrassed. 'Sorry to be in your way. I have to observe this afternoon. See how it all works.' He held out his hand. 'Jonathan Sandford. I'm an inspector.'

'Oh,' I said, taking his hand and feeling slightly unnerved by his presence. I sat down at my desk and glanced at Eva, who winked at me and then chewed thoughtfully on her pen while I rearranged my papers. Jonathan extracted his magnifying glass from his pocket and began to write on a small pad.

'What are you writing?' Eva asked, the pen still in her mouth.

I glared at her.

'Just describing the set-up. The queue, the desks, you two.'

'What are you saying about us?' Eva asked, tipping her head to the side and running her tongue over her teeth. I tried to kick her under the table and she grimaced at me.

He looked at her in surprise. 'Well, if you must know, I'm writing that one of you is chewing a pen and not wearing any shoes . . .' he paused and his eyes flicked over towards me, 'and that the other of you has the biggest eyes I have ever seen and traces of tea on the left side of her upper lip.'

Eva laughed and I rubbed my hand over my mouth. 'Do I?' I asked.

He grinned and nodded just as the door of our office opened and the first appointment of the afternoon was ushered in. Eva and I were obliged to stop snorting with laughter and to adopt our usual pose of administerial efficiency.

I saw him watching me during the day, making small notes on his pad and reading through our books of appointments and registrations. He walked with a limp when he went to fill the kettle during our tea break and, as we sat on the windowsill with our mugs of tea, he told us that he had trodden on a mine in Belgium at the beginning of the war and there were still bits of metal in his leg. He lifted his leg and shook it, and asked if we could hear it jangling. Eva laughed when he did that, pushing her ear to his leg. I sat next to her, absently twisting my mum's old wedding ring that I wore on my left hand at Vivien's insistence.

'Is your husband away?' he asked abruptly, looking at my hands, Eva's head still resting on his ankle. She looked up at me, suddenly serious, shaking her head slightly.

I had a sudden urge to tell him everything. I wanted to tell him everything that Eva knew. I wanted to tell him about the night in the park. I wanted to tell him about Vivien's face when the doctor brought me back that night. I wanted to tell him about the bandages I used to bind myself in when I went to work until it hurt too much to continue, and about the bitten fingernails

178

of the chemist who gave me pills which were supposed to stop the vomiting. And I wanted him to know about Michael, and about the letter I got from Michael. I wanted him to know everything.

But I didn't tell him any of those things.

Not then. Not ever.

Instead it was Eva who spoke first. 'Stevie's husband died two years ago,' she said simply. 'She doesn't like to talk about it.'

I looked at her in surprise. She continued to look straight ahead, defiantly avoiding my eye.

'I'm sorry,' he said.

I nodded and drank my tea and when I stood up to take the mugs back to the kitchen I saw Eva grinning at me and I thought that maybe she was right. It was not the truth, but it was a version of the truth. And, as Vivien was forever reminding me, I had Emily to think of now. I needed to be more practical.

At six o'clock, as Eva and I put on our coats, he got up too and left his books neatly in a pile on the chair where he had been sitting. We followed Eva down the steps, and the three of us walked together towards the tube station at Elephant and Castle. Blackout blinds were being fastened across the windows of the houses and our shoes squelched along the pavement. Barrage balloons floated above us in the sky.

He left us at the corner of Walworth Road, stopping so suddenly that my cheek bumped into his shoulder. And there it was again, that smell. He shook hands with both of us as our bus approached and Eva nudged me as he turned to leave.

'Mr Sandford,' I called after him. I hesitated when he

turned around because I did not know what I wanted to say. 'Are you coming back tomorrow?'

He looked at me and nodded, and I felt Eva's hand on my elbow, dragging me excitedly onto the bus.

But, when I try to remember him now, it is with those dark smudges always across his face.

Michael

It was one of Laurie's favourite topics of conversation, the manner in which the noble domestic pigeon had been flapped inelegantly from its deserved podium as the harbinger of evolutionary theory, and replaced by a gaudy bird from the Galapagos. In classic racist tradition, according to Laurie, the innocent rock-pigeon was demonised and forgotten, and the glory of Darwinism was instead laid at the unwebbed and fleshless feet of the finch.

But this is not how it happened. It was whilst picking through the amateur pigeon collections of the eminent and late Mr Wicking, Mr Tegetmeier and Mr Bult that Charles Darwin first conceived of his curiously irreligious theory of the origins of man. When I leafed through Laurie's leather-bound copy of this study, it struck me that the most remarkable thing about it was not its cataclysmic impact on the superstitious bent of rural England but its demonstration of one man's boredom threshold reaching so great a height as to threaten permanent retinal damage to those who strained to look up at it. Darwin's study of pigeons is tedious in its thoroughness. It is the work of a man who liked to make lists.

Darwin listed pigeons under groups, races and sub-races. He listed differences occurring in the respective lengths of the rear end of various fantail pigeons. He measured the capacity of the conical beak of the short-faced tumbler bird. He marvelled at the range of oesophagi found in the pouter pigeon. He counted vertebrae and compared the correlative size of eyelids with that of wattled nostrils, the sternum and scapula with the furculum.

And, Laurie told me with delight, when Charles Darwin met his cousin Emma Wedgwood, he took out his notebook and made a list of her marriageable qualities and compared them with a list of attributes that undermined his inclination towards marriage as nothing more than whimsical foolishness. He calculated probabilities of happiness and subtracted these from the reduction in productive scientific output that might be the result of such a union. He summarised his findings in a table that he folded into an equilateral triangle and kept in the breast pocket of his velvet smoking jacket for a year and two months.

It was the depth of the first set of these studies that finally persuaded him that all pigeons had, in fact, descended from a single breed of pigeon and that perhaps this theory could have a wider application among the earth's fauna. This fact being irrefutably confirmed in his mind, he later set off in *The Beagle* and only then did he espy the Galapagosian finch.

So you see, it was the pigeon that started it all. Laurie and I treated our pigeons with the respect they deserved. When pigeon conscription, of a sort, was implemented across Allied Africa at the end of 1941, Laurie decided that I should go with the birds. I left the farm laden with grain and a crate of muscular birds and delivered them personally to the head of the Pigeon Service branch of the Royal Corps of Signals in Cairo, a certain Mr Fred Strachan. Mr Fred Strachan had an abnormally large head upon which he had precariously balanced his peaked Captain's cap. The delicacy of this cap's position prevented him from making any sudden movements, a prohibition that permeated his whole being. When he smiled, his mouth leaked across his face like melting butter. His heavy eyelids seemed to shudder as he lowered them into a blink and, when he looked at me, he rolled his thumbs around each other as if they were set in treacle. I arched my feet inside my boots and asked if I could join the Pigeon Service.

I was put in charge of developing the night-flyers at the Training Centre in Cairo. I was to impart my knowledge to a group of lads from the North of England, who were later to be sent on operational service in Italy and the Middle East. I would lecture my new recruits on Darwin as we waited for the pigeons to return from dawn training flights, and they would talk amongst themselves in voices that were dusty with soot and made me think of Alf.

We found that night-flying was not a genetically transmitted characteristic of pigeons. It cannot be measured or inherited. The ability of any bird to fly at night is entirely dependent upon its emotional stability. Pigeons never lose their fear of flying in the dark. We picked birds upon whom the trauma of being tossed into the cloudless nights of Cairo had only a marginal effect. We chose sturdy, shallow pigeons with dry eyes. We taught them to fly upwards rather than along, away from the shadowy trees and sharp telegraph wires that contributed to our greatest losses. We released the young

183

ones just before dawn so that they could fly into the light.

I grew fond of Cairo. It was dusty and white and busy. We were stationed in an old hotel with cobwebs spiralling grandly out of moulded corners. I had a room to myself with a window overlooking a mosque. I would sing along to the early morning call to prayer and roll over in my sleep so that I was facing Mecca.

I spent two years at the training centre before being dragged reluctantly into operational duty. The movement of the Allied troops through Italy after the fall of Tunis meant that more training was needed on the mobile lofts that were being developed on the Adriatic coast. I was attached to a Highland regiment and was offered a selection of rifles and grenades. I refused all offers of guns and instead requested a motorbike for transporting pigeons. A 250cc Triumph arrived for me with an instruction booklet on how to perform the various stunts that I had seen the despatch riders doing in North Africa. I put the booklet in my pocket and tried to find second gear.

I kept my pigeons in a large wire-netted cage with detachable legs. I had to provide messenger birds to all the men who were sent on ill-planned missions behind German lines whenever there was radio silence. The land on the German side was heavily mined, and I would try not to think of the battalions I had already seen disappearing in shards of camouflaged metal. We would wrestle the pigeons into cut-off socks so that only their heads were visible and the lads would make me put one in each of their pockets so that they didn't have to touch them and I would issue instructions on how to release

184

the birds if they were needed. The eyes of the boys would glaze over and the birds would return the next day with upside-down message bags and bloated stomachs.

Only one of my pigeons was ever decorated for bravery, a hen called Queen Matilda. Queen Matilda was a pale feathery hen with furry legs and a throaty cough and was the only bird to return from a troop of thirteen who had been sent on a reconnaissance air mission in early 1944. She fell sideways onto the floor of the loft with a thump, salt clinging to her toenails and stinging her eyes, and a message attached to her leg telling of a plane shot down near Brindisi. The other pigeons had gone down with the aircraft but Queen Matilda had managed to peck her way out of the damaged cage as it was sinking, and had then turned to the surviving men and demurely offered her leg. The men composed a message rambling with coordinates and declarations of love, and Queen Matilda flew over sixty miles of stormy seas to bring it back to the loft.

I took the piece of paper gently from her leg and tapped it through to HQ, and when I turned to pick her up I found that she was stiff in my hand. The five men who had sent the message were rescued from the middle of the Adriatic and Queen Matilda received the posthumous honour of the Dicken Medal, for what it was worth.

Anna puts the Dicken Medal back into my shoebox and tells me that there is talk of the government buying a hawk to circle Trafalgar Square in an attempt to reduce the number of pigeons.

I sigh crossly at the ignorance of the ruling classes. They should read some Darwin.

Stevie

Jonathan's parents lived in a white house with mock Tudor beams running diagonally across the front of it. Inside, the house was filled with light. It shone from tasselled velveteen lampshades and was reflected in gilt-edged mirrors. It danced in the owl-shaped crystal ornaments that were lined up along the window-sill, and imprinted itself on thick carpets in diamond-shaped patterns of leaded light. There were heavy knives and forks that glinted extravagantly in drawers, and symmetrical ceramic displays on the side-board.

As soon as we arrived, I knew I was out of my depth.

Jonathan's mum looked at me in surprise when I took my shoes off in the porch. I hadn't noticed that she was still wearing hers. Her fingers were squeezed into gold rings that looked like they would have to be cut off if she ever decided to remove them. The flesh of her fingers bulged over their shiny sides and I felt the hard-ness of the metal pressing into my palm as we shook hands.

We sat in the living room and I squinted politely at the photographs of various family members and the framed cuttings of cross-stitch above the sofa. There were small squares of toast arranged decoratively on the teatray.

I caught Mrs Sandford eyeing my ankles. 'Stephanie,' she began loudly.

I looked up.

'Did you do ballet as a child?'

'No,' I said.

'I find,' she continued, 'that one can always tell a ballerina from her ankles. There is something delicately Russian about a ballerina's ankles, wouldn't you say?' She lifted a leg and twirled her foot extravagantly.

'I'm afraid I couldn't say,' I answered, uncertain whether she was expecting me to describe her ankles as Russian. 'I don't know any ballerinas personally.'

Jonathan's mum flapped her hand at his dad, who was slumped in the folds of his knitwear. 'Roger, wouldn't you say that Stephanie has such English ankles? Roger!' she barked.

He looked up with a start, knocking his pipe off the arm of the chair. I looked at him questioningly and tilted an ankle accommodatingly so that he could get a better view of them.

'Mother,' Jonathan interrupted, 'why must you always go on about people's ankles?'

'Oh very nice. Very nice indeed,' Jonathan's dad said sleepily, nodding encouragingly at me, evidently unaware of what he was supposed to be saying.

I took a piece of toast from the tray and bit into it. It had a thin covering of rhubarb and ginger jam, which made me cough in surprise. Jonathan's mother looked at me in dismay. I shifted in my seat and asked after

Jonathan's sister. It transpired that her ankles were very Eastern and she had a lovely new coat.

Nobody mentioned Emily.

After the war ended and just before I married Jonathan, I enrolled Emily in a ballet class run by a White Russian emigrée dancer called Irina Gordievsky. I sat on a wobbly wooden chair at the back of the hall and inspected her ankles. They were decidedly delicate. She had extraordinarily long neck bones and her hair was scraped off her face into a bun that sat defiantly on the top of her head. She seemed to be in a permanent state of fury, which she directed most frequently in the direction of the elderly man at the piano. I considered this to be a natural consequence of having her hair constantly dragged back. It must have given her a terrible headache.

The pianist was called Oleg and had fat yellow fingers that shook when he lifted them to turn the pages of his music. He wore a nightcap on his head with a large white bobble on the end of it that he would toss dramatically over his shoulder before starting a piece. He wore cardigans and corduroy trousers and red slippers that jittered under the piano stool. He had a strong penchant for the opening movements of Shostakovich's Seventh Symphony and would work these into the piece that he was playing wherever possible. Irina considered Shostakovich a Stalinist and glowered at Oleg whenever she heard him striking the irreverent opening chords.

'Not this Communist racket!' she would shout, stamping her heels into the ground as she executed an enraged *pas de chat*. The troupe of small girls under her command would copy her, stamping and looking sideways as they continued to dance in their thermal vests and grey knickers, uncertain which bits were for them and which bits were not. The effect was like a comic music-hall production.

Oleg would ignore her and shut his eyes, muttering loudly in Ukrainian whilst continuing to play his Communist music. I learnt later that Shostakovich was spending his nights on the landing outside his apartment so that his family would not be disturbed should Stalin's police come for him when everybody else was sleeping. When he was eventually denounced and forced to repent for his unpatriotic formalistic composition, Irina softened towards the Seventh Symphony but her relationship with Oleg remained volatile.

In the gaps between routines, I saw Emily trying to catch my eye across the room. I tended to ignore her. I justified this cruelty by convincing myself that she would thank me one day, when she realised why she was there. It wasn't for the ballet. I didn't care if she never managed to perfect her execution of a *chassée* or hold an arabesque for the required length of time. I was ambivalent about the physiological benefits of walking on pointes, and I didn't mind if she had certificates to prove it or not. It was what the lessons represented that mattered. Ballet lessons, piano scales, French pronunciation. They all represented the same thing. Choices. Opportunities. That's all. I wanted her to have more choices than I had had. I didn't want her to end up working in a factory. Isn't that all that any parent wants?

So I continued to studiously avoid her eye, and whispered that I would get her a quarter of an ounce of sugar-coated pear drops from the sweet shop by the station on our way home if she was good.

She didn't ever thank me. I didn't really expect her to. But she forced Anna to do ballet lessons too, bribing her with more sophisticated sweets and electronic devices than I had done and proudly distributing small photographs of Anna dressed in a lemon tutu with a cross face, arms splayed awkwardly, and her toe pointed at a slightly pompous angle.

That is the photograph I keep in my purse, the one that makes Anna irritable when I show it to uncomprehending, powdery visitors who are politely dismissive. Of course, they don't realise what it is I am showing them.

Michael

The farm was full of butterflies when I arrived back on my motorbike bearing a battered crate of shell-shocked pigeons. I lay on the grass and listened to the sky fluttering above me and watched as Laurie took each bird out and turned it over in his hands before putting it in the shed.

There were three of us in the household after the war; four if you counted Peter, which Laurie did and Mollie didn't. Neither of them counted Kenneth, Mollie's old houseboy, who insisted on sleeping on the veranda and who would periodically disappear to Nairobi without warning and then slope back days later, his pockets stuffed with pamphlets.

Mollie was a lady from the neighbouring farm who had moved in while I was away, and had taken over the organisation of the coffee-planting. Her husband had died in the middle of a field of unpollinated almond trees and her farm had been repossessed so Laurie had invited her to live with him. She called it a marriage of inconvenience and then rolled her eyes at Laurie for his refusal to play along with the joke.

Mollie had long silvery hair that was heavy with pins. I never saw her hair hanging free from this complicated arrangement. She held her head very straight, and you could see the weight of it pulling on her neck if she made any abrupt movements. She was thin and tall and wore glasses on the end of her nose, and dressed impractically in white blouses buttoned up to her neck and huge skirts that swung around the heavy army boots that she strapped to her feet.

She would sit by the fire with me and Laurie in the evenings, telling us long stories about summer fruit competitions and amateur dramatic productions in Nairobi. She knew all the gossip about the new settlers who came after the war, the cockneys who screamed at spiders and couldn't tell a python from a grass snake, and who thought that Kenya would make them rich.

She read aloud to us from out-of-date British newspapers, and we heard from her about the first session of the United Nations and about Gandhi's pilgrimage of peace. When she informed us of the School Milk Act in England I thought of my parents and looked away. She cut stories from the local newspapers and stuck them into notebooks that she kept in a battered trunk that we were not allowed to touch.

'What are you keeping them for?' I asked her.

'I am writing a history book,' she announced grandly, 'on the Fall of Empire.'

Laurie snorted.

She looked sharply at him. 'You can't keep pretending that this will last forever, Laurie. There are rumblings already. And anyway, I thought you were a republican. Or is that just the pigeons?'

'Of course I'm a republican. I'm not marching around like some Black and Tan, am I? I just live here.'

She tilted her chin obstinately. 'Well, I still think there are rumblings,' she concluded darkly, and returned to her meticulous snipping along the edge of a newspaper report on the identity card protests in Mombasa.

I resumed my post as Peter's assistant in the kitchen and the principal shit-scraper in the pigeon shed. Peter had recently inherited a pair of glasses from a distant uncle, along with two goats, and he had taken to balancing the former precariously on the bridge of his nose. He wiped them with the fraying heel of an old sock, leaving paisley patterns streaked across the lenses, and adjusted them whenever he didn't know the word for whatever he wanted to say in English. He twirled them at women and straightened them at men. He waggled them at small children and tapped them when he wanted to get my attention. They became his largest feature, swamping his smile and hiding his eyes.

He would bend over the chopping board, clicking his tongue at the way I was slicing melons, and the glasses would slip from his nose into the slushy pile of melon seeds. We retrieved them from carrot soup and coq au vin, stuffed peppers and shepherd's pie, and eventually he agreed to attach them to a string around his neck to prevent any further culinary mishaps.

He was politely disdainful to Kenneth who, when he was traceable, was occasionally sent to the markets with Peter's shopping lists. I remember how Kenneth would lurk at the side of the room while Peter sucked his teeth as he unpacked the cheeses Kenneth had bought in Nairobi, all the while berating him for his choice of vegetables.

'How am I supposed to make a proper English roast when you bring me only chilli peppers and chickpeas?'

Mollie looked around the kitchen door. 'You should listen to him, Kenneth. He cooks like an Englishman.'

'Better,' I added.

Peter beamed proudly and Kenneth moved aside to watch him, listening resentfully as Peter told him how mushrooms ought to be stuffed with cream cheese and not eaten just as mushrooms, and that only a madman would think of serving fish without lemon. As Peter grated the zest of an orange into an Irish stew, Kenneth leant forward and angrily whispered something I did not understand into Peter's ear in fast Kikuyu, and I saw the uncomprehending look in Peter's eyes as Kenneth stalked out of the kitchen.

And later that evening, for a confused and silent second, I saw the way Peter looked at Laurie as he handed him his dinner, before he blinked and smiled.

I wondered if that counted as a rumble or just a beginning.

India was granted independence during the pigeon-breeding season of 1947. Peter twirled his glasses in excitement and asked if we could call the new pigeons after the Kenyan nationalists instead of Irish ones. Mollie went to retrieve her 'History of the Fall of Empire' and flicked through its sticky pages. She read out names of leaders of the Kenyan African Union which Laurie then wrote into his pigeon ledger underneath his roll call of increasingly obscure Irish nationalists.

When we had finished, Mollie coughed tentatively until she had everyone's attention, and then announced that she had decided to leave Kenya. She said that she had no intention of being driven into the sea by a machete, and besides, she was getting arthritis in her knees. Laurie told her she was being ridiculous, but Mollie merely nodded and turned to me.

'What about you, hmmm?' she asked, prodding me with her finger. 'What do you think? Will you accompany an old lady back to the Motherland?'

I rubbed my hand over my face. 'I don't know.'

'You can't stay out here forever,' Mollie said, looking closely at me. 'Why are you here? What is it you're hiding from?'

I shook my head. My secret was still stuck, lodged into my flesh like a bullet and I could feel it under my skin when I ran my hands guiltily over my body at night.

Laurie looked at Mollie. 'He can stay here if he wants. Wars are not easy on the internal organs. He will have his own way of recovering.'

I felt the muscles of my arms twitching, and imagined hands holding me. I had not considered the possibility that I might be recovering. I looked up at Laurie. 'Maybe I should go back,' I said. 'Would you mind?'

'Of course I wouldn't mind. It's up to you.' He turned away from me and walked out of the house and down to the pigeon shed, and when I went to find him he was sitting on the roof in the place where I usually sat, holding a tiny Jomo Kenyatta in the palm of his hand.

'Laurie, I don't know how to ever thank you . . .'

'Then don't,' he said. 'Just remember you're welcome here if she won't take you back.' He grinned at me, and I wondered how he always knew everything.

Mollie took charge of all the arrangements. She filled box after box with books and bicycle parts and china plates that she wrapped in old copies of the *East African*

195

Standard and which she left on the veranda for me to pile into the truck. She gave away her frilly blouses with their high collars to the local Kikuyu women, who shrieked with laughter when they tried them on. The floor of the house became shiny as it emptied. And once the last lid of the last box had been nailed on, Mollie and Laurie took me apart too, limb by limb, and gently packaged me up and sent me back to England in a box marked FRAGILE.

Stevie

On my wedding night, I fell asleep with my nose squashed into Jonathan's armpit and I dreamt I had been swallowed by a whale.

We were married in the Registry Office in the summer of 1945. I wore a pale green cardigan over a cream dress and Jonathan wore a dark grey suit with a yellow tie. My mum sat on a low stool at the back, colouring in pictures of pirates while Emily sat on her knee, patiently devouring the Order of Service. Jonathan's family sat on the left-hand side of the room and were dressed all in black. I heard his mum whispering noisily to his sister about the lights being so bright that it made my dress look white, and they both tutted darkly at the very prospect.

Afterwards, we went back to Vivien's house and there were crispy sausage rolls and sandwiches with no crusts, and fairy cakes with butterfly wings that Emily and I had made the day before. The shelf next to Jonathan's mum had an accusing finger-shaped streak running through its thin layer of dust, and it shone in my eye when I went over to offer her another sausage roll.

Jonathan and I spent our first night together in Brighton. We drove down to the coast after the last of the cakes had been eaten, leaving Emily drowning in a sea of crumbs and ribbons at Vivien's feet. Our bedroom had a four-poster bed with salty pillows and flapping curtains. There was a swarm of seagulls living in the rafters who jabbed at the windows all through the night. It felt as if we were living at sea.

The first night was terrifying. I lay as flat as a window-pane and considered how big Emily had been when she came out. I ran my hands over Jonathan's back, lingering over the strange lumps of muscle that I didn't have. When it was over I curled myself up as small as I could manage and rolled timidly into him. He wrapped himself around me, holding me close, and then promptly fell asleep. I lay awake for hours, wide-eyed and uncomfortable, my bladder pressed into my stomach, too embarrassed to move. I was terrified of disappointing him.

I wondered if he had known it would be like this. He asked me to marry him under an umbrella in Walthamstow after a visit to his sister. The rain was bouncing off the pavement and up the backs of my legs and I was thinking about how wet my stockings felt inside my boots. It was 20 August 1944. The Russians had just clumped into East Prussia and General de Gaulle was powdering his nose on the outskirts of Cherbourg. We were almost at the end of everything.

His umbrella was half-broken and spiky and it poked me in the ear when the sirens went off. There were doodlebugs everywhere, slipping through the wet sky like huge silvery fish. Flashes of lightning hung silently above us and we counted the gaps until the thunder as we ran to the public shelter.

There was a queue of flat-haired people waiting to get

down, water dripping from the ends of their noses and adding to the puddles on the stairs. An old lady had fallen and was blocking the way, and people were prancing crossly and excitedly over and around her. She was complaining that a tin of mustard had rolled out of her bag and she refused to move until it had been found. An elderly, cardigan-shaped man had nearly persuaded her not to worry about the mustard when he was interrupted by a devastating crash. It sounded as if a roll of thunder had fallen out of the sky and landed in the middle of Walthamstow. The man dropped to the floor and buried his face indecorously in the lady's lap. She put her hand on the top of his head and held it there, stroking it softly, her eyes continuing to cast around in search of the errant condiment. Jonathan and I crouched in a doorway, still on the pavement, his umbrella balanced on the tops of our heads.

And that was when he said it.

'Marry me.'

An emaciated dog started to sniff at my ankle. I jumped. 'Pardon?'

'Marry me. When this has finished. Marry me.' He looked desperately serious, and was almost pleading with me. I tried to ignore the dog. Its nose was scratching against my calf. I shook my leg, attempting to dislodge it.

'But Jonny, what about Emily? I mean, it's not just me.'

'I know. Of course I know that. I'll love her too.'

Too? It was not something he had ever said before. And I hadn't ever said it to him. There was something else I needed to know. 'What about me?'

He began to laugh. 'Do I love you? What a question!

I think you're the bee's knees. I always have. Isn't it obvious?'

I shook my head. That sort of thing is hardly ever obvious. But then I began to nod, a smile creeping across my face. No one had ever called me the bee's knees before. I was glad he hadn't just said that he loved me. Anyone could say that.

'So, is that a yes?' he asked.

I carried on nodding. 'Yes, it's a yes,' I said and flung my arms around his neck, knocking the umbrella out of his hand so that it fell. I heard the dog yelp as it landed in its eye. The rain came and planted itself wetly all over my face and lips as we stood and held each other so tightly that I thought I might break.

I don't remember falling asleep that first night. Our wedding night. I remember noticing how his breath came in waves against my neck and that his body was as warm as sunlight, and I watched how easily he fell asleep. I felt a surge of envy at his mastery of this basic skill. I was still an amateur sleeper, unskilled and restless, and customarily assaulted by a range of recurring and exhausting dreams.

As usual, it was only when I woke up in the middle of a dream that I realised I had not been awake all night. It was a new dream, which was unusual, and it was surprisingly gentle, given the turbulence of our maritime room. In my dream, I had been consumed and filtered into one of the stomach chambers of a blue whale, washed down by a huge wave of sea water. I spent the night swishing against the sides of the stomach, my elbow bumping against an old pram with no wheels while oblivious fish swarmed purposefully between my fingers and over my toes. I made my way across to a slimy lump of blubber which was just above water level and I heaved myself onto it. It moulded to my body shape, cradling my head and folding warmly around my shoulders. I spent the rest of the night basking in its indifferent softness, lulled by the gentle rocking motion of the whale. Molluscs attached themselves to my arms, and a small pool of water gathered in my stomach. I felt irresponsible and safe. I woke up with my eyes stuck together and my skin shiny with amniotic fluid.

Years later I read about other people who had been swallowed by whales. My favourite one was swallowed whole in 1891 and was cut out from the stomach of the whale onto the deck by the rest of the ship's crew two days later, hungry and colourless and slightly mad. I read in one account that, on his return to England, he was exhibited at a museum in Plymouth and people paid a shilling to look at him. He reminded me of when Anna used to demand tubes of Smarties in sweet shops and then sit at the dining table and diligently suck the colour out of each of them. She would put the sucked Smarties back into the tube and offer them delightedly around and we would pretend to be surprised at their whiteness. I pictured him standing there beneath a sprawling explanatory sign, sucked white and cracked at the edges and oozing soft chocolate.

Then there is Jonah, obviously, but everyone knows about him.

I remembered this dream while I was at the library the other day. I left my place by the large-print fiction section (I was on to the Js) and decided to look up the modern research on how best to survive being devoured by a whale. I had to ask the librarian where to start. She had a squeaky voice and was sporting purple pyjama trousers and a headdress of dirty blonde dreadlocks that got trapped in books when she shut them too abruptly. She was nonplussed by my dilemma and seemed irritated to be called away from chewing her nails whilst staring vacuously at the Local Studies section.

The results were not altogether helpful. It seems that even today, in this age of space exploration and long-distance telephone calls, there is still no tried and tested method of absolutely guaranteeing a foolproof escape from a whale. According to the latest scientific research, swallowees who have been fully devoured ought to try to cling to the front of the tongue and hope for a fortuitous gap in the teeth, but the constant battery of sea water tends to cause most candidates something of a problem. Another marine biologist suggested that, in theory, an effective method would be to light a small fire at the side of the mouth and try to smoke your way out. However, he did concede in a footnote that this method was unlikely to meet with much success, for obvious reasons. This same self-professed expert also advocated the technique of lining the whale's throat with freshly ground pepper and hoping to be sneezed out. I was not impressed. I returned to the large-print section with a diminished opinion of marine biologists and decided to skip *Ulysses* in favour of some short stories.

I had the same dream for each of the three nights we spent in Brighton and each morning I woke up to find myself wrapped in Jonathan's arms. By the end of the second day I had learnt to walk around semi-naked in the toe-stumping darkness and Jonathan had not yet shown any obvious signs of disappointment.

In the mornings we ate black pudding and baked beans in the dining room of our guesthouse, and for lunch we ate fish at wooden tables that wobbled on the pebbles of the beach. We spent the afternoons in grand hotels, sipping schooners of sherry and gawping at the chandeliers. On the third day, I won a shower of pennies on the one-armed bandits along the pier and we spent them on ice creams that dribbled over our hands and onto our feet and left creamy trails behind us on the boardwalk.

Being by the sea made my eyes water and the skin tighten across my face. I yawned constantly. We walked hand in hand for miles along the edge of England breathing in the exotic Sussex air. We passed narrow rows of blue-painted shops filled with messy wooden shelves and I bought a small globe for Emily that had a carpet of grey seagulls lying at the foot of the Brighton Pavilion. When you turned it upside down the Pavilion was revealed to be standing in the sea and the gulls took flight and fluttered erratically until they landed once more, belly-up and wide-eyed. Jonathan thought it was morbid. I thought Emily would like it.

We spent the evenings in glassy rooms with darkened sea views, eating shepherd's pie. On the last night Jonathan looked at me strangely and asked me if I ever thought about Michael.

I was in the process of lifting a cup of tea to my mouth. My little finger sprang up in surprise and the tea sloshed over the side of the cup. The spillage distracted me and

I wondered if Jonathan would consider it ill-mannered to drink tea out of a saucer. I was still a little uncertain as to the finer points of tea etiquette.

I thought of Michael's letter cutting into my hand. I breathed in. 'No,' I said.

'I just wondered. You make strange noises in the night and I just wanted to know.' He looked at me. 'You can tell me if you do think about him. I don't expect you to forget all about him. I would just have to try harder not to mind.' He smiled as he said it, but the wrinkles around his eyes didn't show.

I tipped the tea from the saucer carefully into my cup. 'It was a long time ago,' I said. 'I don't like to talk about it.'

I should have told him then. I should have told him everything. But I just shook my head and Jonathan looked away, hurt that I did not trust him enough. But it was not that. I did not trust myself. I did not want to think about it.

I thought then how Jonathan had never asked me if I loved him before we got married. I remembered the rain falling on the umbrella, the pain in my knees as we crouched under it, the smell of Walthamstow burning. I put down my teacup and swiped for his hand under the table. 'We were just children, me and Michael,' I said. 'It's you I want to be with now. I think you're the bee's knees too,' I told him shyly.

I was surprised that it had taken me so long to realise it. You have to understand, I was a product of my time. We all were, us factory girls. Not for us the tortured purchaser of the self-help manual. We were part of that aspirational post-war generation of abandoned women who craved security and electric washing machines with a bottomless desperation. We didn't know how to say no.

He smiled and squeezed my hand softly.

Later that night we fell a little less awkwardly into the bed that we were learning to share and pressed our bodies into each other. The curtains were open and the moon was shining brightly in, shimmering brazenly against my bare skin. When he rolled away from me, I arranged myself diagonally across the mattress with my arms resting on the pillow above my head. He wrapped himself around me and once again I watched him fall expertly asleep.

And, later still, I too fell asleep to the sound of the sea and the pecking of the gulls at the window, and once more I dreamt I had been swallowed by a whale.

Michael

Mollie and I travelled back to England by boat and arrived in Liverpool in October 1947. Mollie was to move in with her daughter who had a farm in Oxfordshire, and I was going back to my father's dairy. I slept fitfully on the train down to London, my head resting against the window, and woke to find that the bar of chocolate in my pocket had melted onto the side of my seat. I scraped at it as the fields faded into the edges of the city. From the train window I could see small houses huddled together in clumps, interspersed with dewy rubble.

I stood outside Euston station for a while, trying to remember which bus I should get. It seemed that England had developed pointy elbows while I was away. It jabbed me rudely in the ribs and jostled the metal-framed bag on my back. Men with frayed pockets and unhemmed edges refused to lift their eyes from the floor as I walked past them. There were no bananas or proper eggs, no windows and no books. I had not appreciated how easily dirt collects in corners.

It was raining in London, a pathetic sort of rain, half-hearted and quiet, with the persistence of a small boy tugging at a sleeve for attention. At the bus stop, I held my tongue out to catch the drops and the end of it turned grey as the rain soaked into it. When it came, even the bus was dripping on the inside. Water ran down the insides of the windows and formed droplets on the ledges. People slipped on the stairs. Children smeared the windows with their fingers, writing their names backwards in the condensation. The conductor held his nose in a permanent wrinkle of disdain. I blew into my cupped hands and played with the buttons of my new raincoat.

I was reluctant to go home. I had written a short letter to my parents from the farm after Mollie and I had decided to leave, apologising for my silence but offering no explanation. I gave them details of our journey and must have mentioned that Mollie and I were spending our last night in Kenya at Whitesands Hotel in Mombasa, because when we arrived there was a telegram waiting for me at reception from my father. It informed me that the house next to ours had been bombed in 1944. He had been in bed at the time, still refusing to go to the bomb shelter and they found my mother's body just outside the house next door. She had been hit by a falling window on her way to the shelter. He had signed the telegram 'Love F'. I imagined my father walking grandly down the stairs after hearing the crash and standing there, not too close, long and thin and half-dressed, waiting for the fire wardens to arrive. I wrapped my scarf more tightly around my neck and shut my eyes, and when I opened them again I found that the bus had stopped and we were in Lewisham bus garage.

The conductor shuffled along the aisle and tapped me on the shoulder. 'Cigarette?' he asked, holding one out to me.

'Thank you.' I followed him to the end of the bus and

we stood on the platform at the back, holding onto the metal pole between us. We smoked in silence, listening to the rain hitting the sides of the bus, until he took a final drag and flicked his cigarette out across the depot. I looked at him, and he gestured with a flick of the head that I was to do the same.

'You going back the same way?'

I nodded.

'Why didn't you get off the first time?'

I looked at him and shrugged. 'I wasn't ready.'

He nodded and I crawled back to my seat. The bus growled northwards once more, from Catford to New Cross and then turning towards Elephant and Castle. I stared out of the window, trying to remember where one thing fitted into another. As we shuddered along the Old Kent Road the air on the bus began to smell of burnt peanuts and I looked up in surprise at the half-fallen walls of the Sun Pat. I grabbed the arm of the conductor as he passed. 'When did that happen?'

''41,' he answered gruffly.

I stood up, and slung my bag over my shoulder.

'Getting off?' he asked.

I nodded dumbly and he stretched his arm above his head, plucking the bell wire. I jumped onto the pavement and looked at the remains of the factory, and wondered where I would find Stevie now.

I turned away and walked towards the dairy. My father was eating a cheese sandwich over a plate of newspaper when I arrived home. He stood up and then sat down again, gesturing towards the chair opposite him. The table was smaller than I remembered.

Eventually he spoke. 'I wasn't expecting you until

tomorrow. You should have said you were coming. I'd have made you a sandwich.'

'That's okay. I'm not very hungry.' I coughed awkwardly and put my bag on the floor. 'How are you?'

'Oh, you know.' He had a crumb on his cheek and I watched it moving as he ate. 'How about you?'

'I'm tired.'

He nodded and I put my bag onto a chair. 'Here.' He slid the newspaper over to me and watched me devouring the rest of the sandwich. When I had finished he took a deep breath as if he were about to say something important. He held his breath for a while.

I smiled flatly, expectantly, until I realised that he didn't have anything to say. I helped him out. 'How's business?'

He nodded and sucked the crumbs ponderously from his fingers. 'Getting better now. Everything's getting back to normal. We only lost one cow. The brown one.'

'Graham,' I said.

'What's that?'

'Graham. That's what Mother called the brown one.'

'Oh. I didn't know that.' He furrowed his eyebrows slightly and shrugged. 'But other than that, everything's the same really.'

I looked at him and wondered how he could fail to notice that everything had changed entirely. 'Except for Mother,' I said quietly.

He nodded his head for a while as he looked out of the window. 'Yes. Except for your mother. I'm sorry.' He reached out and patted my arm. I did not look at him but left my arm there, allowing it to be patted. My mother's absence was obvious and loud and there was something different about my father. The war seemed to have blown his anger out of him, but now that it had gone, he seemed transparent. There was nothing underneath.

'Anyway,' he stood up, 'I'll get some sheets ready for your bed.' He smiled nervously. 'In the front bedroom, if that's alright with you.'

I nodded, slightly surprised that he did not sleep in the bedroom he had shared with my mother. 'It's fine. I'll do it.' I stood up and pulled at the knot of my tie. 'You finish your tea.'

'Oh.' He grabbed my elbow and tweaked it awkwardly. 'Thank you.'

I took a bundle of sheets from the cupboard and stretched them over my parents' old bed in the dark. My father was brushing his teeth and gargling in the bathroom. The curtains were dusty and already drawn and I wondered if they had been opened since my mother died. The bulb flashed and died as I clicked the light switch. I pulled open the curtain so that the room was filled with a soft yellow light from the streetlamp outside. There was a knock on my door and my father slid his fingers around the catch as he pushed it open.

He hesitated and cleared his throat. 'I forgot to say, there were some letters. They were returned here because they said you'd been demobbed.' He gestured vaguely around the room. 'Your mother kept them somewhere.'

I stared at him. 'Letters?' I repeated.

'Yes.' He looked at me as if he had only just noticed I was really there. 'You look ill.'

'I'm just tired,' I said, removing my clothes from my bag and laying them out on the chair next to the window.

He nodded. 'I'll find them tomorrow for you. It's too late now.'

'Okay.'

He went to leave the room but then turned suddenly and asked, 'Were you demobbed then?'

'Only for a while. I went back.'

He pressed his lips together in satisfaction. 'I thought they must have been wrong. Otherwise you'd have come home, wouldn't you? That's what your mother said too.'

I smiled and my father took this as an agreement and left the room. I sat down and opened the drawer next to my mother's bed where I knew she kept the pictures and old birthday cards that Ben and I had made when we were little. It was her hiding place, where she knew my father never looked. He was put off by the prospect of finding suspenders and thermal vests. They embarrassed him, her undergarments, even when folded in beige piles.

I recognised the letters I had sent from Catterick at the beginning of the war, and later from Nakuru. They had been folded neatly and kept in order. I took them out and put them on the floor and pulled the drawer out further. There was a child's painting which I did not remember either Ben or I having made that I also removed, and underneath that, at the back of the drawer, was a bundle of letters held together with an elastic band. I picked them up and turned them over. They were all addressed to me, unopened and faded.

I put them back in the drawer and lay down on my mother's side of the old bed, her counterpane spread over my legs and her reading glasses lying carelessly on the table beside me. The lenses reflected the light from the streetlamp into my eye so I turned them to face the other way. I thought of how my mother wore them on the end of her nose, peering over them when she looked up from the newspaper, attached to a string around her neck. They always made her look so much older.

I shut my eyes for a moment and listened to the noises from the street outside, cars and voices and footsteps, and then I sat up again and opened the drawer. I took out the letters and turned them over, propping myself up and adjusting the angle of the pillow so that the yellow light from the window fell on the paper. I ran my finger along the seal of the first envelope, breaking it open. I could hear my father's hisses coming from Ben's bed in the room next door.

I began to read.

Stevie

I leave the library at dusk, a collection of large print Ms under my arm. The air smells of hairdryers and peeled potatoes and the bus stop is misty with deodorised spray. I struggle onto the plastic bench of the shelter, and let my legs swing below me. People crowd in front of me, their eyes glinting competitively, and I wonder when queuing fell out of fashion in England. People do not expect to wait for things any more. They like immediacy, promptness. It used not to be like that. Impatience was tolerated only in temporary bursts.

When Jonathan and I were first married, I found the days incredibly long. Jonathan would go to work and I would take Emily to school, and then I would spend the day washing sheets and wringing out shirtsleeves until Emily was ready to be picked up from school and Jonathan came home again, hungry for his dinner. I was not used to preparing more than one vegetable at a time. I was accustomed to huge vats of food in the factory canteen and Vivien's immaculate cooking. My attempts were laborious and the results were runny and too soft.

I tried desperately hard to be grateful but the repetition of it bored me. I started going to the cinema during the day. I swapped casserole recipes with my neighbours

213

and sat half asleep while they recounted stories of their children's progress and the digestive habits of their cats. I walked a lot and joined committees. I learnt to play badminton. I went to museums and made notes on a clipboard.

It was almost inevitable that my mind would start to wander.

Occasionally, I would find myself thinking about Michael. His last letter had been posted from Nairobi so I thought perhaps he was still in Kenya. I borrowed an atlas from the library and traced paths across it with my finger, returning it reluctantly after two weeks, only to take it out again the next time I passed by. I bought picture postcards of baobab trees and piles of spices in blanket-draped market stalls from a small shop that I found in Bromley Common and stuck them on the insides of the kitchen cupboards and wondered if Michael had seen all the things I had seen.

I began to write secret letters to travel agents requesting brochures of Africa. They sent me icy pictures of French mountains with purple skies and window-framed pictures of marble-flagged churches in Rome, giving details of tours of relic-encrusted crypts. I imagined the head of St Pancras peering out from an underground wall. I read the brochures at night, running my fingers over the pictures, and showing them to Jonathan who was obligingly attentive.

And under our bed I kept a separate pile of brochures of places I knew I would never visit. I collected yellow pamphlets on thin paper in colonial fonts, advertising hunting safaris in Africa and trips to the New World. They had dusty pictures of sailing boats on the Nile and black men dressed sparsely in faded cloths with spears and glassy smiles. There were pictures of white women in frilly blouses and hollow helmets with nets hanging over their faces, and they would stand in groups with men who had rolled their socks over their knees and had rifles hanging over their shoulders, all of them squinting at the camera.

A travel agent opened up optimistically near the station, and I found that it took hardly ten minutes longer for me to walk back from Emily's school via the station. I would look in the window, scanning the shelves for new brochures that I hadn't already acquired. The man behind the counter would look expectantly over his glasses at the nose that was dirtying his window, and when he saw it was only me he would look away again. His wife was more understanding. She would point out new brochures and regale me with long-winded stories about customers who had been on holiday to Greece and had suffered from irregular bowels ever since. All her stories ended up with some strain of digestive trouble and a shake of the head.

I began to dream that one day I would go into the shop and buy a ticket to Africa. I imagined myself sitting on a boat surrounded by the Red Sea, somewhere watery beyond Port Said which I thought might have been on the edge of Egypt. In my imagination, the Red Sea looked the same as the English Channel at Brighton. I would have a burnt nose and a pith helmet on the shelf above my bunk, like Isabella Bird or Mary Kingsley or some other Victorian explorer. I had never been to sea, never even left England, but still I dreamt of Africa.

Naturally, Vivien announced there must be something

wrong with me when I confessed this new obsession to her. She said it wasn't normal to want to go to Africa, and I thought she was probably right. I didn't feel normal. I felt impatient and nervous. I cried over spilt milk. I didn't sleep at night. I lay in bed with my hands resting on my stomach, Emily stretched out on the pillow between me and Jonathan. She slept with her finger in her tummy button and climbed higher and higher up the pillow as she slept until her head rested on the wall behind her. And I would feel Jonathan's arm lying heavily across me, reaching across both of us, holding us in. I was so nearly happy. There remained only a tiny some-thing, something unexplained and inexplicable that buzzed in my ear when the lights were out, like a malarial mosquito.

On our second wedding anniversary, Jonathan nervously presented me with a map of France and a heavy book with a red-leather cover containing lists of French towns and pencil drawings of water mills and churches. He told me that I could choose where I wanted to go and that he would take me there. I looked at his eyes, trying to see if he had guessed about the mosquito.

We bought a passage on a P&O ferry leaving from Dover and took the train from Calais to Chartres. I spent the journey exclaiming at shop signs and looking out of the window at small farmhouses interspersed with rubble and scaffolding. When we arrived in the town we ate pork cooked in cider in a small café. The café had pitted walls from which you could see the spires of the cathedral where the Resistance fighters had hidden from the Germans. The original stained glass had been put back in the windows and, but for the jagged remains of a statue that had been shot down from one of the towers, you could almost forget there had been a war there at all.

The next day we went to the cathedral, and I stood in the middle of the nave and stared upwards for so long that when I came out the sun blinded my eyes and I couldn't see anything. I thought Jonathan had gone without me and I realised that it was no more than I deserved. I sat down where I was on the cold stone of the cathedral steps, and put my head in my hands and decided that enough was enough. I pressed my hands over my ears and when I looked up again and saw Jonathan waiting for me at the bottom of the steps, I found that the mosquito had finally gone.

After that, I buried my pile of brochures in the bottom of my half of the wardrobe in our bedroom, and I stopped dreaming about Africa. I mopped up the spilt milk without a second thought. I helped with reading at Emily's school and was sometimes left with a whole class all to myself and I would stand marooned on the teacher's platform, grinning inanely. I was no longer waiting for anything. I lay next to Jonathan as he slept, and every night before I fell asleep I would brush my nose against his arm to drink in the smell of him.

Emily's house is dark when I get back. I turn on the radio and sit next to the window so that I can see Emily's car when she pulls into the drive after picking Anna up from the hospital. I close my eyes and wait.

You see. It was just a phase.

217

Michael

I have something to show you.

'What is it?' Her shift has just finished and she is buttoning up her coat.

I reach under my pillow and bring out a small silver thimble. She looks at it and says, 'It's a thimble.'

I shake my head. *It's a kiss,* I write.

She laughs. 'Like in *Peter Pan.*'

I nod.

'So who gave it to you?'

I hold the thimble out to her. She takes it from my trembling hand and puts it on the end of her finger, and then I give her my notepad so that she can read what I have written.

'You had a daughter? Where is she? Why haven't you mentioned her before?' She takes the thimble off her finger and looks at it.

She doesn't know me. Her mother married someone else.

'Why?'

I was in Africa.

'Why didn't she wait for you?' she asks defiantly. 'She should have waited.'

I shake my head vigorously. *No. I don't blame her. It was*

all my fault. I told her . . . I stop and scribble out the words. I am forgetting myself.

Anna looks closely at what I have written and then looks at me. I shut my eyes so that she will not see all the things that I desperately want her to guess.

It didn't take long to find her. I saw a girl on Rye Lane who had worked in the canteen with Stevie, and she nearly jumped into the street when I tapped her on the shoulder. She told me that Stevie had moved to Bromley with her husband after the war and my feet clotted in my shoes.

'She's married?'

The girl nodded. 'Do you want her address?'

I nodded dumbly, and the girl scribbled the name of a road onto my bus ticket.

I went to Bromley that afternoon and sat in a pub on the corner of her road and waited. I didn't want to scare her, arriving too abruptly. I didn't want to see him either. There was a clear panel of glass through which I could watch the road with my left eye whilst appearing not to be spying. The rest of the window was frosted and stained. There was not much activity until about three o'clock when, just as I was getting up to go to the bar again, I saw a door opening on the opposite side of the street. I stopped and put my eye to the window.

She was wearing a red cardigan with a bow that tied at the side and a dark grey skirt. I had forgotten how small she was. I had forgotten again. I grabbed my coat and followed her up the road, wondering what I should say. She crossed the main road and turned left down a smaller road, and then turned in at the gate of a school, exchanging nods with the other women who were beginning to congregate around the railings. I stood back against a wall and watched, straining to hear what she was saying to the woman next to her. The air was clammy with smudged fingers and clunking pianos. A pigeon came and stood by my feet and I bent down to pick it up, holding it against my chest so that I could feel its tiny heart fluttering.

I saw a small girl come out of the gate and run to Stevie, and I saw Stevie kiss her on the cheek. My fingers pressed against the ribcage of the bird. I could feel its lungs, its liver. I opened my mouth to call out to them but nothing came. Emily. I mouthed her name. My daughter. They stopped at the corner of the road and Stevie bent down so the girl could climb onto her back and wrap her legs around Stevie's waist, leaning forward as she did so and describing things excitedly with her hands as they walked. I watched them go and clutched the pigeon to my chest.

I went back to the pub the following afternoon and saw Stevie and Emily coming back from school. I bought another drink and read the newspaper and waited. It was dark by the time I saw him returning from work. Her husband. He was tall and thin and walked as if his toenails needed cutting, and when she reached up to kiss him at the front door I felt the bottom drop out of my stomach.

I spoke to him the next day. I stopped him as he turned into the road to ask for the time, not because I needed to know but because I wanted to hear his voice. I thought it might give me some sort of clue, a small insight into her life now. All I learnt was that it was half past six and he didn't have any sort of speech impediment, which I found mildly disappointing.

They had a house with a green gate that had to be lifted as it was opened, otherwise it scraped along the ground and got stuck on the uneven path. I looked through their windows when they went out and ran my fingers along the pebbledash. They had a brown settee with cream cushions and a gas fire and a photograph of Emily on the wall.

Now that I had found Stevie I could not leave her again. I wanted to know that she was safe. I wanted to see if he carried her bags and helped her with the gate and made her laugh. I didn't ever want to see him touch her, but I found myself imagining it all the time and the thought of it obliged me to turn around and attract the attention of the barman with a swift jerk of the thumb towards the gin bottle.

After I had been watching them for about two weeks, I arrived at the pub just before one o'clock on Saturday. He left the house not long after I arrived. Stevie left about an hour later with Emily. She was carrying a basket and wearing a blue dress that swung around her knees as the two of them galloped along the road, Emily honking with laughter.

Normally I stayed in the pub when they went out. I wasn't ready to talk to her. I didn't want her to turn around and see me. But that day I followed her all the way into town and to the park next to the library and I sat down on a bench, still keeping my distance, my neck aching as I watched her around the curve of the hill. Stevie took a rug out of the basket and laid it on the ground, and then took out a book and started reading. Emily lay on the rug, immersed in conversation with herself.

I hardly knew what I was doing. I began to walk over to them. As I got nearer I saw the flat freckles on the backs of Stevie's hands and the splits of her toes where they disappeared into the ends of her pumps. She was wearing a gold ring on her left hand. That was new as well. I tried not to look at it. She had flecks of grey in her hair and she was wearing silver earrings that sparkled in the sun. She used to say she thought earrings were common. When she looked up at me her eyes were that same shade of bright blue that they had always been when she smiled. When she *really* smiled.

She stopped smiling when she recognised me. She dropped her book onto her lap and stood up quickly and then sat down again.

We did not speak at first. We just looked at each other, concentrating. I didn't want to be distracted by talking. I wanted to memorise every little line of her, every freckle and every mole, every shadow on her face. I wanted to count her eyelashes and take her pulse and check her teeth for cavities. I wanted to breathe her in and press my head into her chest.

I don't know how long I stood there, forgetting to breathe, my cheeks turning red from lack of oxygen. Stevie stood up carefully and took a step towards me. Emily stopped counting and joined in our new game. She began to stare at me too. 'Who are you?' Her words exploded noisily between us.

I looked down at her and tried to explain but nothing came out. It was Stevie who managed to formulate a word first. 'This is Michael,' she said, hurriedly. 'And Michael, this is Emily. My daughter.' She tried to say it casually, but it came out defensive, possessive. 'She's six now. She was six in June.'

Emily nodded proudly and began to run in a circle around us.

I suddenly thought I might cry. 'I'm so sorry,' I whispered. 'I didn't know.'

Stevie stared at me. 'But I wrote to you. I sent you hundreds of letters.' She looked around her, behind me. 'Where's Tabitha then?'

I shook my head desperately. 'It wasn't like that.'

'Why did you . . . ?' She tailed off, her eyes narrowing, and then whispered, 'You promised me you'd come back to me.'

'I didn't know what I was doing,' I was gasping now. 'I can't tell you what it was like out there. I can't tell you what I did. It was awful, Stevie.' I reached out to touch her arm, but she backed away. Our eyes held each other until she sniffed quietly and looked away.

I dragged my eyes away from Stevie and glanced down at Emily. She looked nothing like me. She was wearing a red and white striped dress and had blonde hair that was cut jaggedly across her forehead. She had resumed the game she was playing in the grass. She was counting loudly to herself. I was surprised that she spoke. I didn't know much about six-year-olds.

'She cut her hair herself,' Stevie said eventually. 'I don't know why. I came in and found her hacking away at it and swooning at her reflection in the mirror.'

I laughed nervously. I imagined the mirror, a three-sided mirror with hinges that swung round so that you could look in your ears and at the back of your head. I used to be intrigued by the back of my head. And there would be a little stool to sit on, with a padded seat that matched the carpet and maybe cleft hooves on the ends of its three legs made by a Germanic-looking Irishman from County Cork.

'You can speak to her if you like,' Stevie said.

I bent down and tried to join in. She put her finger to her lips in impatient indulgence of my interruption. She was at seven hundred and eighty-three. She continued for a while and then picked up the thimbles from the rug and growled *eight hundred* at me with an air of resigned finality.

I asked her if she could show me how to play her game.

She sighed and told me that she thought it was too difficult to explain.

'We could play Peter Pan instead,' she suggested, graciously. 'I'll be Wendy and you can be Peter.' She looked at me crossly. 'Go on then, be Peter Pan and pretend you've lost your shadow.'

I saw a half-smile flicker across Stevie's face. I put my hands on my hips and wondered how to fly. I had just got my happy thought all ready and needed only a small sprinkle of fairy dust to set me off when I heard someone calling over to us, well, to them, from the bottom of the hill. It was him. I recognised him straightaway. There were three oranges tucked in the crook of his arm and he was carrying a rolled-up newspaper in the hand that he was waving.

Stevie caught hold of my arm. 'Michael! You have to go. I'm sorry.' She stopped. Her fingers were bony against my arm and her face had turned shiny and red. She lowered her voice. 'I told Jonathan you were dead.'

I fell out of the sky. I had lost my happy thought. And now I knew his name and I couldn't forget it again.

When Emily saw Jonathan, her interest in me faded with remarkable rapidity. My skin felt transparent and speckled, like a hot potato. She began to run in circles again.

Jonathan disappeared momentarily as the path wound around the side of the hill. It was my last chance. 'Stevie, I'm so sorry. I wrote that letter because I did something terrible. I couldn't come back.' I was gasping now. There was too much to say, too much to explain.

'I don't want to hear about that,' she whispered.

'You don't understand. It's not what I said it was. I only told you about that because I did something else, something terrible. And these . . .' I began to drag her letters out of my pocket, waving them at her, straightening them out to show her the things that she had once written to me. 'They sent them to my father. I didn't get them. I didn't know until now.'

Stevie did not take the letters that I held out to her. She simply stared at her feet and wrung her hands in front of her as if they were soaking wet. 'Put them away. Please.'

I folded them reluctantly into my pocket. Jonathan's head appeared again around the side of the hill. He dropped an orange and stooped to pick it up.

I said again, 'I'm sorry.'

She nodded and placed her book back into her bag. I pawed at the grass with my foot. She bent down and rolled up the rug and, without looking at me, she said,

'I loved you. I'd have waited for you forever, but not after that letter. Only a fool would have waited for someone who told them what you told me. And I had Emily to think of.' She put the rug in her bag. 'I loved you,' she said again, very quietly so that Emily would not hear, and then she lifted her eyes to mine and, in that brief second, I saw that she would have forgiven me.

I felt a tug on my trouser leg. Emily was standing next to me, her head tipped coyly and her cheeks flushed. She was holding a thimble in her hand. It was sitting upright in her palm, like a tent. She held it out to me.

'It's for you. It's a present.'

'What is it?' I asked her.

'It's a kiss, of course,' she said scornfully.

I turned it over in my hand.

My daughter folded her arms and sighed at my ignorance. 'Wendy gives one to Peter Pan, remember,' she elaborated. 'He doesn't know what one is so she gives him a thimble and tells him it's a kiss.'

I nodded. I had forgotten that bit. I curled my hand around the thimble and held it tightly. I noticed that Emily's ears were asymmetrical and one had a very slight dip in the top of it that looked as though someone had taken a bite out of it. I ran my fingers over the tip of my own ear and felt where it dipped. I wanted to scoop her onto my knee and read *Peter Pan* to her and find out why Wendy gives him a kiss, because I didn't remember it being a love story. But instead she began to gallop sideways towards Jonathan, and her voice came in waves as she went, instructing me to read the whole book again because she kisses him properly nearer the end and that maybe I had forgotten that bit too.

Stevie bent to pick up her bag, her eyes glittering. I offered the thimble for her to take. I wasn't sure if I should give it back.

'It's for you. Keep it,' she whispered, and she reached out and touched my hand gently with her fingers and then turned her back slowly and walked away, towards her husband. She stopped after ten measured paces and I thought she was going to turn around and look at me as I was looking at her, but instead she reached down and took off one of her pumps. She shook the pump and bashed its heel against her hand, and then slipped it back on and carried on walking away from me. She was limping slightly as she walked. But still she didn't turn around.

She has seen me since but I don't think she recognises me. She glances at me and I see her wondering for a second but she does not know who I am. I have changed, after all.

As I made my way home, I rolled the thimble around my hand, trying it out on my fingers to see which it fitted best. Mollie had taught me to crochet in Africa so now I made a small woollen pocket to keep my thimble in, somewhere safe and warm to keep my daughter's kiss. I tied the pocket to a piece of string and wore it around my neck like a hippy. It was small and grand all at once, and it was all that I had.

I leave out the names when I tell Anna. I tell her only small bits, and she looks up at me after she has read each instalment.

So you see, I met my daughter only once and she gave me a thimble.

Anna smiles and touches my arm. 'I think it's a lovely story.'

I reach for her hand.

'No,' she says, 'I can't take that.'

But I push the thimble into her palm and close her fingers around it. I shut my eyes, and when I open them again she has gone.

Stevie

I saw Michael twice after the war. The first time I saw him he didn't see me. The next time I didn't see him until it was too late.

The first time was in the café in the Army & Navy Stores. He was in the corner of the restaurant, in a booth next to the window. He looked older than I remembered him, and his clothes lay awkwardly on him. His hair was thin and had turned blond, and there was a scar on his cheek that folded like a dimple when he moved his mouth. He looked like an elbow patch on a tweed jacket, battered and obvious, and not quite whole.

He was on his own, facing towards the window. I hid behind a pillar and undid the collar of my blouse and rubbed my shoes against my stockinged calves so they were a bit shinier. I pinched my cheeks to redden them. I could feel my heart beating against the sides of my stomach.

I peered round the pillar. His jaw was clenching visibly, bulging inside his cheek as he lowered a teaspoon into his cup. I remember that, the way he would fill the spoon high with sugar and then sink it slowly into the heavy mix of milk and coffee, letting the white grains discolour slowly and melt from the outside in, until they were floating above the spoon in the liquid. He let the spoon fall and began to stir quickly. I remember how I sat with him, watching this small ritual, feeling like a child because I couldn't reconcile the soft smell of the coffee with the bitterness of its touch on my tongue. His leg was bouncing restlessly under the table, making the cup shiver on its saucer.

I stepped back so that I could no longer see him, uncertain what to do. My hands felt big and awkward. I tried tucking them under my armpits, squashing my chest beneath them. I tried slinging them into my pockets, so that my skirt bulged to the side, but they no longer seemed to fit.

In the end I folded my arms behind my back, each hand gripping the opposite forearm and stayed hidden behind the pillar, keeping an eye out for cat-like women who might be called Tabitha until, eventually, he stood up and brushed his hands down the front of his trousers, and walked out.

I let him go.

I met Jonathan in the hosiery section as we had arranged and rested my head against his arm as we walked and still I did not tell him. I breathed him in and felt the warmth of his body against my arm, and I knew I would never tell him because I did not want him to leave me.

The second time I saw Michael was just over a week later in the park near our house. I was there with Emily. He must have seen me first because he was already walking towards us by the time I recognised him. I couldn't think of anything to say. My head tipped like a bucket and emptied completely. I heard it gushing out of my left ear.

He stopped in front of me and I stood up. I felt my hands prickling against each other. He looked at me, locking me in. I couldn't tell what it was that I saw in him. Guilt, surprise, expectation. His cheeks were blue where he hadn't shaved and his hands were light brown and hairy. He smelt of warm beer and dried tobacco.

It was Emily who spoke first, bouncing up to us and shouting for attention. I managed to remember the things that other people say. I introduced them to each other, as if we were adults at a tea party and I began to ramble about Emily's hair. And I thought to myself as I talked, *Is this the best I can manage? Nearly six years and this is all I have to say?* The words continued to drop from my mouth onto the grass between us, fully formed and ridiculous.

He didn't say anything. My wedding ring clung pointedly to my finger and we both avoided it, as if it were an unsightly boil. He watched Emily for a while and she was bossy and impatient with him, which he seemed to like.

But there was something wrong with him that I couldn't put my finger on. I wanted to wrap my arms around him and hold him together. He looked over his shoulder all the time and spoke too quietly. We stood together and watched Emily running in circles in front of us. Once he bent down to shoo away the Canada geese that came too close to her, fussing at them with the stick he carried. He tapped his foot on the ground and his hand against the bench and his fingernail against his teeth. He took short, deep breaths. The taps gave the impression of words being said, but I didn't know what it was that he wanted to say. A pigeon landed close to him and he went as if to pick it up, but it flew away just as his hands were about to close around it. Emily stared at him in surprise.

A child in a tree behind him was swinging upside down from his knees. His ears were starting to go red at the tips where the blood was collecting in his head. Michael was trying to tell me something about the war, something he said he should have told me. I always thought Tabitha wasn't a real name. He reached his hand out to me and I could feel my flesh rising to meet him, the blood threatening to burst out of my skin. His finger-tips brushed the edge of my coat.

He almost had me.

Suddenly a breath of recognition passed across his face and he let his arm drop. I turned to look behind me. It was only later that I wondered how he had known who Jonathan was. Perhaps Jonathan had waved but I had missed it.

Jonathan's limp was more pronounced from a distance. I felt suddenly and fiercely protective of him. He was carrying oranges and waving a newspaper. So there it was. I had to make my choice. When I looked back the boy in the tree had gone.

In retrospect, I suppose I already knew what I would do. I had made my decision as I stood behind the pillar in the Army & Navy Stores. I leant towards Michael and whispered, 'I'm sorry, Michael. I'm sorry. It's too late.' Perhaps I said something else too. I don't remember. 'Leave us alone. Please.'

I can still hear the cracking noise that came from his

stomach when I said those words, like a cream cracker being broken in two. He didn't seem to notice it. He began to whisper frantically, his voice stuttering and falling over itself, telling me that he was sorry and that he wanted to explain something to me.

But, like I say, it was all too late. I had already become practical, even then. As early as 1947. I had stopped believing in stories. It was all just stories. I didn't want to hear his new story. Did he not think that I might have had a story too?

'Please. Just go.' Was there anything else? Or just that. *Go away*. There might be something I'm forgetting, a feeling I can't quite put my finger on. I remember walking away from him. I made myself look straight ahead, drowning in the huge mugfuls of air that swilled heavily around my lungs like milk. I didn't look back once.

No, wait. That can't be right. I did look back. I remember stopping, bending down, doing up my shoelace or adjusting my stocking. Michael was backing away, so slowly that I could still have called out to him and he would have stopped and everything would have changed forever. I watched him surreptitiously through the crook of my elbow as I crouched down. Everything waited, just for a moment. The leaves turned red as they held their breath. Worms poked their heads out of the soil and craned their necks towards me. The clouds sunk a little lower, straining to hear.

'Stevie, are you okay?'

I looked up and saw Jonathan hurrying to help me, the sun behind him as it always is when I try to remember him now, eclipsing his face. I straightened my laces and smoothed down my stockings, and then I stood up and continued towards Jonathan. The leaves let out their breath and fell from the trees, swirling carelessly around my feet. I had let him go again. And it was easier than the first time.

Michael

When I walked out of that park, I decided to disappear completely. I was a little unsure as to how it would work. I thought disappearing would be difficult and time-consuming but, in fact, it was easier than I had envisaged.

These days, there are companies that offer disappearance advisory services. Perhaps there were in my time too. I just didn't know where to look. I notice them everywhere now, hidden among adverts for second-hand lawnmowers and dubious 'No Win No Fee' lawyers. Disappearance Consultants. Skip Tracers. Alternate Identifiers.

A few years ago I sent off for a brochure, just out of curiosity, and I received in return a suspicious-looking package from America. It claimed that the best hiding place for a fugitive was a certain corner of desert in the south-western states, and offered to arrange transportation for a small fee. I hadn't thought of that.

The brochure continued by delving into the minutiae of a runaway's life. It advised against licking stamps and envelopes, advice that didn't seem particularly relevant for someone who is attempting to disappear completely, and warned of the dangers of sitting on toilet seats without paper protection. It insisted on the destruction of all photographs. No goodbyes. Clothes to be cut into jagged squares and flushed down the toilet. Hats should be worn indoors at all times to prevent the escape of stray hair follicles, soap checked for pubic hair, attachments formed with large groups of motorcyclists or other sidelined delinquents. Never lift your eyes above mouth level. Drink from straws and flush them down the toilet. Only ever walk downstream.

Some of these companies even offered traps to throw people off the scent: a knife dipped in a small pool of blood and left carelessly poking out from under your bed. And then there were the disclaimers. No guarantee of total disappearance. Tax advice extra.

But, like I say, it was easy for me. The aforementioned suggestions are based on the supposition that you are actively being sought. This was not a problem in my case. My disappearance was understated in its simplicity. There was nothing elaborate about it. It was entirely uncontested.

Don't get me wrong. I don't blame them. I don't even blame her. How could I? But I am just saying.

I am just saying that it is remarkably easy to disappear if you put your mind to it.

I found lodgings in London with an acquaintance of Mollie's nephew. My room had a tiny window and a sloping roof and was balanced precariously on the top of the house. It had a coarse carpet that I found comfortingly solid, and velvety green patterns on the wallpaper that reminded me of Brendan's hallway. I got a job as an electrician at Lewisham Hospital, the hospital I am in now, and spent my days negotiating the back corridors with their industrial lifts and fire escapes, checking ECG machines and replacing flickering neon bulbs. Nothing much has changed since then. The walls are still off-yellow and the nurses' shoes still stick to the floors.

In those days, my landlord was rarely at home. He worked in the City, writing numbers in ledgers that he occasionally brought back to the house and which I would leaf through when he was out. He had a shelf of crystal glasses that he kept next to the television, and which I would fill with spoonful after spoonful of gin, diluting them only slightly with the warm tonic water that I kept under my bed to give an illusion of decency.

I became fluid and hard to contain. Too loud for polite company; too erratic for everyone else. I spent evenings tuning my spectrum scanner to the same wavelength as the neighbours' telephone lines so that I could get to know them a little better, and listening to police radios on shortwave. I perfected the art of patience, and kept a collection of tennis balls stuffed down the side of the sofa to throw against the wall when I became frustrated with the paucity of entertainment on the television.

I began again. I kept my money in a brown paper bag under my bed, and once a month I took it to the bank and paid it in, until I had enough to buy a small house in Lewisham with a shed in the garden to keep some pigeons. I experimented with the effects of cortisonal steroids administered to the eyes of my birds and found that I had become a minor celebrity in the pigeon-racing communities of south-east London.

Laurie arrived on my doorstep in 1964 after having read about my pigeons in the *Pigeon Post*, shivering in a thin cotton shirt and carrying four muddy boxes of exotic plant cuttings, and asked if he could stay with me for a while. He conceded that Mollie may have been right about the rumblings, but he refused to go back to Ireland. He was still a republican, after all.

'She didn't take you back then?' he asked.

I shook my head. 'I was too late.'

He grunted and looked around him. I shifted slightly on my feet as he ran his eyes over the steroid drops on the mantelpiece. He raised his eyebrows at me, which were even longer now than they had been when I last saw him.

'For the birds,' I explained. 'Makes them go faster.'

'I know,' he said. 'But it's bad for them. You shouldn't use it.'

'Oh,' I said. I handed him a cable-knit jumper and he pulled it on over his head. 'What do you think you'll do over here?'

He looked at me, pushing the sleeves of the jumper up his arms. 'Landscape gardening. Mollie sent me an article about it. She says it's all the rage on the Green Belt.' He pulled a crumpled page of a magazine from his pocket and held it out to me. 'The cuttings in those boxes will be worth a fortune.'

I liked having Laurie there. He emptied the pigeon eyedrops into the bath when I was not looking and I stopped drinking as much. My pigeons became more alert, if a little slower. We entered them into grand races and commissioned oil-based portraits of them which we hung in the living room. We named them after the presidents of Africa and we grew mangoes next to the pigeon shed. We played Scrabble together at the pub and built a fireplace in the living room.

But, although we never talked about it, Laurie knew there was somewhere else I liked to go when I was not working at the hospital or attending to the pigeons with him. Every day, or as near to every day as I could manage, I went to the pub opposite Stevie's house and I kept watch over her and over Emily.

I was there when the Russians put a man in space and when the Communists locked the Brandenburg Gate in Berlin and when the Beatles landed in America. I was there when a man wiped the remnants of a fried chicken wing from the edges of his mouth and pointed a gun at JFK, and when the American ping-pong team went to play in China. I was there when Brixton went up in flames and when the Berlin Wall was taken apart piece by piece.

And, more importantly, I was standing behind a pillar at the back of the church when Emily married the thin-haired man who kept his eyes open as he kissed her at the altar. I was there when my granddaughter was wheeled round to visit her grandmother and her grand-mother's husband for the first time. I was there when that same man with the flickering eyes left my daughter. I hobbled from the pub as I saw him leaving the house and stepped off the pavement just as he released the handbrake of his car, hoping that he might hit me and be imprisoned for dangerous driving. I hoped that my daughter would see me and smile vengefully from the window, but he braked too soon and swore at me like the fool that he is, so I only managed to make a slight dent in his bonnet with my stick as a parting gesture.

I transferred to work at Farnborough Hospital to be closer to my daughter. Four times a day I went to the third floor to check the bulbs on the optometry ward where she worked, and I rushed to hold doors open for her. Occasionally she would smile at me, not knowing who I was, and on those days I would feel the buttons of my overalls straining over my bursting heart as I walked home in front of screeching cars and swaying buses, just as my father had done before me.

What I don't tell Anna is that when I found out she was working as a healthcare assistant in the thoracic cancer ward in Lewisham, I shut my eyes and clasped my hands so tightly that my knuckles ached, and I prayed that if I was going to have to die of anything, please God, let it be thoracic cancer.

It is funny, the prayers that get answered, and the ones that don't.

But you see, I was always there anyway. Watching. And waiting. Keeping her safe. Keeping all of them safe. Stevie. Emily. Anna.

I leave out the names when I tell Anna. I stop and look at her. Her head is tilted to the side. She squints at me and I wonder if she has guessed.

'Which hospital?' she demands. 'Where did you used to work?'

I shake my head. I cannot tell her.

She changes tack. 'Where's Laurie now?'

He died. Four years ago.

There is a clump of mascara in her eyelashes. I watch it moving as she speaks. 'Did you ever speak to her? Your daughter, I mean. Or your granddaughter?'

No. It is better like this.

She reads what I have written and looks at me, her fingers worrying the thin part of her dented ear. I will not look away until she blinks. But she does not blink.

Stevie

It was the toenail incident, as it later became known, which Emily claims propelled her into becoming an overly cautious child. She does not like to be thought of as cautious, suggesting as it does a lack of spontaneity, a want of impulse. She thinks she is odd. She does not remember the way Vivien always extinguished candles with a spoon because she worried that blowing them out might dislodge the hot wax into somebody's eye. She does not remember the bicycle clips her grandmother wore whilst walking to the shops, in case she tripped over the ends of her own trousers. She does not realise that her cautiousness, if not exactly inherited, had been drummed into her from an early age, pressed onto her in the years when she stayed at home with Vivien while I worked at the Ministry. She does not see that the toenail incident was a blip. It was a moment of disorder, of small mutiny, coming as it did two days after Vivien died of a heart attack in the room next to Emily's, before things were restored.

She lost her toenail when she was ten years old, a minor casualty incurred during the Great London Smog. At precisely the same moment as an Aberdeen Angus cow keeled over at Smithfield, spluttering sulphur dioxide, and a young man in a mustard-yellow raincoat fell into the Thames by mistake and drowned, Emily was running through the kitchen with no socks and a hand-kerchief covering her sobbing face, and stubbed her toe against a chair. Her toenail came off and never grew back, and I blamed myself. I have never been cautious enough. After all, Vivien would never have allowed bare-foot running in a food preparation zone, whatever the circumstances.

I remember the mess it made, the way the blood dried around the toenail so that it stuck to her skin and we had to wait for it to fall off, along with the scab, before we could clean her toe properly. Emily was inconsolable. She wore Vivien's boots for weeks, her foot wrapped in bandages so that it would not fit into her own shoe, unwilling to remove the bandages until the toenail had grown back. But it never did.

I watch her as she sits on the carpet next to my armchair, laboriously wedging pieces of foam between her toes so that they splay as if in shock. I look over the top of the newspaper as she lays a towel out over the carpet and then unscrews the lid of the nail polish. She has four toenails and a soft, white piece of flesh at the end of her third toe, wrinkled like dried glue. She wipes the brush against the bottle, running her tongue around her lips, and then leans forward and carefully brushes red polish over the nail of her big toe. I try to concentrate on the details of Bill Clinton's impending impeachment, but I am finding it difficult to focus. The names confuse me and I am losing all sense of chronology.

'Scott got married last week,' Emily announces

suddenly, bending closely over her knees and wiping away the tiny smudges of red that have run over the bottom of her nail.

'Oh.' I put down the newspaper. 'When did he tell you?'

She moves onto the second toe. 'He didn't. He told Anna yesterday. He wants to sell the house.'

'Oh Emily. I'm so sorry.' I fold the paper onto my lap.

'It's okay. I don't mind.' She pauses and dips the brush into the pot and drips red paint onto the fleshy part of her middle toe, in the place where the nail should have been. 'Oh shit,' she mutters. She spits on the tissue and rubs it against her skin. 'I always do that.'

'Why don't we sell my house instead?' I offer in a sudden burst of entrepreneurial vigour, 'And then buy him out. I'll call the estate agents tomorrow. It wouldn't take long.'

Emily makes a thoughtful noise through her nose and then licks her finger and rubs it against her middle toe. 'No, Mum. It's too soon. For you.'

I shake my head. 'It's fine,' I say. Which it isn't, but this is not because it is too soon. It is too late. I will never go back to that house. It is too quiet, too shadowy. I cannot remember it properly.

'Let's just wait and see for a while, shall we? I don't want to rush into anything.' She tilts her ankle to check for any remaining polish that has landed in the wrong place, and then briefly brushes over the two half-nails on her smaller toes.

I nod, conceding that she is probably right, and Emily moves on to her left foot. I smile as I take up the newspaper once more, my hand reaching for Emily's shoulder. She is just like her grandmother.

Michael

The last message ever transmitted by the French Navy in Morse code was sent in 1997 and this is what it said:
Calling all – this is our last cry before eternal silence.

And then nothing; just a low, soft buzz. So not quite silence. But still, thus did the code of Samuel F. B. Morse slip into the annals of French maritime history.

It is good to have a sense of occasion about endings.

I called a solicitor in to make my will last week. He wore thick glasses and a too-short tie and when he leant towards me I could smell on him the cavernous cellars of the old pubs on Fleet Street. I wanted him to slot me into one of the plastic wallets he kept in his briefcase and file me among his papers and then take me for a final drink, but he didn't even offer. He wore his trousers too high around his waist and spoke from the back of his throat.

He was uncertain whether to disapprove or to sympathise when I told him that I wanted to leave everything I owned to Anna. I could see that he was trying to decide whether I was a dirty old man, or I was acting under duress. Anna came by with her breakfast trolley and I think he must have decided it was the former as she does not seem the sort to go around exercising undue influence over old men. So it is all arranged. It is not for him to question my motives. And, as you might imagine, most people's opinions mean little to me now. He will sort it all out for her when I am gone, and then she can go to university and become a doctor, or whatever it is she wants.

I awake before dawn again today, as I have been doing every day for the last week. The sky from my window is a comforting shade of grey, although it is not the grey that wakes me. It is something else.

My mother swore that she saw an angel when she was little. She had a sister called Bernadette who died at the age of seventeen from tuberculosis, when my mother was six years old. The doctor said that there was nothing more he could do, at which my grandfather grunted dismissively and sent him packing.

On the night the angel came, my mother was sleeping on the floor next to her sister's chair, armed with a sponge and an old medicine bottle filled with holy water that she was supposed to dab in small crosses on her sister's forehead at regular intervals. My grandmother had stolen the water from the font at the door of the church for her sick child and carried it home, blasphemous drops falling between the cracks of the pavement as she walked.

My mother did not hear the angel coming in. She told me she had felt a breeze on her cheek as she was sleeping and when she opened her eyes she saw an angel slouched against the mantelpiece, exuding a damp smell of wet leaves and half-smoked twigs. My mother told me she knew it was an angel because it was white and it was a girl and it looked about the same age as Bernadette, which my mother thought was the right sort of age for an angel. Its arm fell in folds as it reached out to Bernadette, and Bernadette took her hand and stood up as she had not been able to for weeks. The tops of Bernadette's cheeks shone as she walked with the angel into the hall and out of the front door and down the road towards the river. My mother watched eagerly from the window, waiting to see if angels could fly.

It was only when Bernadette and the angel turned the corner and disappeared from view, both sets of feet still firmly on the ground, that my mother crashed disappointedly up the stairs to wake her parents. My grandmother was out of bed in a second. She whirled after Bernadette in a pink cloud of fake Victoria lace and embroidered rosebuds. My grandfather was more deliberative in his pursuit of his eldest daughter, first tucking his shirt into his pyjama trousers and straightening a waistcoat over his upper half before following his wife towards the river.

They found Bernadette slumped against the railings in front of the river, her hands clasped in her lap, holding a flower. She was alone and had stopped breathing. The doctor was summoned to the railings and he pronounced his astonishment that she could have walked this far unassisted, at which my grandfather snorted derisively. My six-year-old mother tried to explain about the angel but nobody would listen to her and she was left bouncing on the grass verge with a huge 'but' smudging the edges of her lips and an unshakable weakness for mystical Catholicism. It was this that later attracted my mother to my father. When she was fifteen, my mother met my father at the church door and he wooed her with his scent of incense and candles, and it was only after they married that she realised his was not the sort of belief that accommodated angels.

He had no sense of occasion.

So here it is. I shall take the letters out of the drawer next to my bed and leave them on my pillow, like a present. I will take the ribbon that Anna wrapped around the jar of my flower, and I will wrap it instead around my pile of photographs and crumpled linen maps of Africa and the bundle of letters. I will scour the ends of the ribbon with the blade of my scissors to make them bounce in childish red curls, so that she smiles when Doreen gives it to her, for even Doreen should know that it is meant for Anna. And then Anna will know everything.

The only problem with this plan is that first I have to retrieve the ribbon from the windowsill and find the scissors and then put the box on the bed. It has been several weeks since I have stood up without any other support. My legs are heavy and reluctant when I attempt to stand and I manage only two and a quarter steps before I fall. I stretch my arm forward and my fingers brush the window.

From my new vantage point on the floor I see a brown-tipped leaf falling from the cherry tree in the hospital grounds. I raise my head a little and I notice then that all the leaves are falling, one by one. I imagine them folding themselves up into neat piles on the lower branches as they land, waiting to be packed into large wooden boxes and stored away in underground rooms.

I picture birds unpicking their nests and lining the twigs up neatly on the soil in descending order of length. In the distance, houses are taken apart, nails hammered out and bookshelves unstuck, and each detail of each room of each house is flattened down and slotted into cardboard flatpacks with instruction booklets and spare nails and sent back to Sweden.

I reach instinctively for my list of mortal sins to comfort me and slowly I begin to unravel them, but for the first time I find that the list sticks halfway and I am no longer sure of the order. Does Fornication come before Murder, or is it after Missing Mass on Sundays? I see Ben's face grinning at me as he lifts the jug of water over his glass, and then I remember and I look around for Alf but I cannot see him anywhere.

I notice with amusement that I cannot feel my shins or my knees or the joints of my toes. My elbows ache where I am pressing on them and I am suddenly and embarrassingly aware that I am wearing my oldest set of pyjamas, with three missing buttons and two thin patches of cotton on the seat of the trousers that make them look almost see-through from a certain angle and in a certain light. I roll onto my back so that the bare bit is covered. The movement exhausts me.

I should have worn my best pyjamas for this.

The sky is almost blue. I rest my head against the cool linoleum of the hospital floor and shut my eyes. My eyelids flicker and I see a golden leaf stuck wetly to the window. And there is something else I can't quite put my finger on. Oh yes. The absence of carrots.

I am tingling all over. The light beats a little gentler against my eyelids and I feel a breeze against my cheek, as soft as a child's breath against a candle on a cake.

A faint hiss of smoke spirals out of my right ear.

And so, in the end, it is easier than I imagined.

Leaving.

... − . −

Stevie

I hadn't noticed the cold setting in until a man dressed as a wolf came to switch on the Christmas lights on the High Street and I realised that everyone else was wearing gloves. My hands were numb and red and there were icicles hanging from my earlobes. The signs above the shop fronts had been overrun with huge light bulbs and the opening of shop doors brought blasts of warm air mixed with tinny voices singing repetitively and unimaginatively about snow.

The news features on the television about the projected number of old people who will perish during the Christmas period have started in earnest. They show the seasonal film reels of old ladies in unravelling knitwear as they struggle onto various forms of public transport. Over the pictures comes the voice of an earnest Northern Irish woman, undulating in that slightly bored intonation that all newsreaders seem to adopt. I flick through my notepad and count that the number of deaths being forecast has risen since the beginning of the week.

I am beginning to wonder if my days are numbered.

I have taken to having custard with everything. I make it thick and lumpy so that it coats my throat and seeps into the cracks of my lightly toasted crumpets and all-butter English muffins. I crumble digestive biscuits into it and spread it onto cream crackers. I have it on the side with Sunday lunch. Emily and Anna are both curious and dismissive. I have tried telling them that it is a recommended recipe for old people and they nod encouragingly. They don't realise that this is what old age tastes like.

I attempt to draw Anna into my custard frenzy. She has just arrived home with red eyes and a battered shoebox wrapped clumsily in ribbons tucked under her arm. She is singing an old Julie Andrews song as she goes up the stairs. She always sings like that when she is upset. Warbling and defiant. I heat some custard in a pan and mix some dried apricots into it and then go to find her.

She is sitting on the windowsill in her bedroom, drizzling gently into the shoebox and rotating a rusty thimble on her thumb.

'Anna,' I say. She looks up at me and I place the custard furtively next to her. She smiles through the mascara lying thickly across her cheeks, like Mary Poppins when she has just popped out of the chimney. 'What have you got there?' I ask her.

Her eyes fix on me. She takes the thimble from her thumb and holds it out to me. 'It's a kiss,' she says slowly. 'Do you remember that?'

I frown and take the thimble from her and suddenly I feel an eyelid opening and shutting inside me. I do remember. I look at Anna and nod, and there is a pause filled with custard. How could she know? She can't know. Of course she can't.

Anna's voice is creamy when she speaks again. 'He died this morning.'

I laugh nervously. 'Who? Peter Pan?' I ask, rubbing my nose and shifting my weight from foot to foot.

She almost smiles but hesitates before it reaches her lips. She takes a deep breath and I think she is going to say his name but then she stops and says quite simply, 'Just a patient.' And then she smiles properly.

'Oh.' I look out of the window. The sky is so blue that it looks almost artificial. Anna is fidgeting next to me. She takes the ribbon from the box and winds it around her finger. The shoebox on her lap is green and scuffed against the whiteness of the window ledge. I run my fingers over the lid of the box.

She looks at me and opens the lid a fraction. There is something familiar about the smell of the box that unnerves me. Her hand is shaking slightly. 'Nana,' she begins. 'There are some things in here that I think you should see.'

I take a step back and trip over one of Anna's shoes and I drop the spoon I am carrying. It bounces under the bed. 'Not now,' I say, steadying myself against the door of Anna's room. 'I don't have my reading glasses.'

'They're round your neck.'

So they are. 'Not these ones. Different ones. These are for different things.' I am being shifty. I know she is watching me. I bend down and reach under the bed, patting the floor to locate the spoon. That smell. I feel memories shifting inside my head, trying to work themselves free. I push them back in, and tighten the string that holds them together.

Anna turns to look out of the window. Her forehead

is creased and she is clicking her tongue against her teeth. 'Would you do something for me?' she asks abruptly.

'Uh-huh?'

'I want to go to his funeral and . . .' She pauses. 'Would you come with me? It's just that I don't want to go on my own.'

I hesitate.

'Please.'

'Alright,' I concede eventually. 'But I don't think I can go in. It's too soon. I'll wait outside, by Granddad's grave.'

She grins triumphantly at me and leaps down from the windowsill, taking her empty bowl with her. She takes the spoon from my hand and leaves the room. I hear her feet landing lightly on the stairs. The radio splutters stoically in the corner. I sit and watch it for a few minutes, and then pull out the plug.

I shut my eyes and try again to remember Jonathan's face. There are still no edges to it. Only dark bits and light bits.

Eventually I get up and follow Anna downstairs and drink a surreptitious mouthful of sherry straight from the bottle, hiding behind the kitchen door. Thus steeled, I tiptoe into the living room and settle myself in the largest armchair in readiness for the *Neighbours* repeat.

I go for a walk while Anna is at the funeral, ignoring the pain in my knees and my toes. I look over the fence into the gardens of the library and watch a thin girl battering a basket of tennis balls over the net with methodical precision. When her basket is empty she collects the balls and stands at the other side of the net and starts again.

I hear the soft vibration of ball against racket strings, and watch the ball landing at the same painted inter-section of yellow lines each time and I wonder if this makes her happy. Is this what happiness is? Repetition? A definite purpose? Having something to grasp at? Is this what I have been missing?

I am distracted by the discovery of a pool of rain balancing precariously on the soft collar of my coat. I hadn't noticed it starting. It requires the execution of a delicate shoulder dip to direct the overflow of rainwater down the arm of my coat instead of allowing it to slither down my back. The girl collects her tennis balls and then zips herself into her jacket.

The service is just finishing when I get back. The church is almost empty but I sit on a chair against the back wall and stand stiffly as the coffin passes. Anna sees me and smiles, and I am pleased that I have come. We wait in a side chapel while the church empties, sitting next to a sign on a tin box declaring that tea-lights may be lit for the extortionate sum of £1.50 each. We run our fingers along the stitching of our pockets in search of elusive coins and between us we manage to cobble together nine-teen pence. We tip the coins into the slot and hear them mingle with weightier offerings and then we each take a tea-light from the pile. I take out my cigarette lighter and light my candle, and Anna holds hers against mine until her wick catches. We put them next to each other at the feet of the Virgin Mary and shut our eyes. I ask forgiveness for having stolen a tea-light and mutter a 'Hail Mary' under my breath.

'He was called Michael,' Anna says.

I start. 'Who was?'

'The man. My patient.'

'Oh,' I say, and I begin to fuss with my bag. My eyes are suddenly blurry and moist.

'It's okay,' Anna says, 'all of it. It's all over now and it's all okay.' She puts her arm around my shoulders and it is thin and heavy and reassuring, and I lean into her and wonder how she can possibly know.

Anna straightens up and looks at the lighter that I am still holding in my hand next to the candles. 'I didn't know you smoked,' she whispers as we turn to leave.

'I don't,' I lie. I glance at the tiny feet of the Virgin, poking out from under her blue dress, before following Anna out of the pew. I add another prayer, for this small white lie. I am sure that the Mother of God would understand, being a mother herself.

We walk home together in silence. I notice how loose my skirt has become and how it seems to reach lower down my leg than it did when I first got it. The rain has stopped and the light has taken on the soft pink of a December afternoon. Anna takes a cigarette from her bag and lights it. She inhales slowly, watching for my reaction, each puff landing softly on my ears and muffling my thoughts. I smile and reach out to her, linking my hand through her arm, and she slows her steps so that they match mine.

We have kebabs for tea. Chicken kebabs wrapped in soggy pitta bread and decorated with green chillies. I feel the sharpness of the chilli seeds against the roof of my mouth, and decline Anna's offer of custard for afters.

*

The next morning, Anna and Emily are talking quietly in the kitchen when I come downstairs to make a cup of tea. An official-looking solicitor's letter is spread out on the table in front of them. Anna is holding the green shoebox on her knee. They stop talking when I come into the room and I see the glance that passes between them. Emily stands up, her dress crumpled where she has been sitting on it, and pulls out a chair for me to sit on and I notice that she is holding the thimble in her hand.

'Mum?' she asks and then stops. There is a soft buzz coming from the refrigerator, filling the space between us.

So there it is at last. They know.

I sit down slowly next to Emily and she slides the solicitor's letter abruptly towards me, and then goes to look out of the window. My feet do not quite touch the ground and they swing beneath me as I read. The words are long and complicated and it takes me a while to understand. Hereunder. Theretofore.

I look up at Anna. 'The funeral. Was it him?' My voice echoes off the soapy plates lined up in the rack.

She nods.

Emily is adjusting things in the dishwasher. 'Why haven't you told us this before? I had a right to know. We both had a right to know.' She shuts the dishwasher too fast and there is the sound of glasses falling against each other. She does not move.

I feel the slats along the back of the chair pressing solidly into my spine and the coolness of the wood against my legs and I rest my head in my hands. She is right, of course. She is always right, my daughter. 'I'm sorry,' I whisper. 'I couldn't.'

The refrigerator continues to buzz, like a fly around an open wound, and there is a heartbeat in my hands and in my head and all over my body in places where it should not be, and I am terrified that Emily will look out of the kitchen window forever to avoid looking at me. But there is only a pause, and then I feel a hand landing softly on my arm. I look up and Emily is standing next to me and Anna is tipping the contents of the shoebox onto the table, and the sun is bright against the window, and there are spotty teacups that I have not noticed before, and the paper of the letter is thick and creamy in my hands, and when at last I begin to speak I wonder why it has taken me so long to find where to begin.

Later that day we drive to Michael's house. It is raining now in huge wet clumps that burst onto the windscreen and the streetlamps are flickering between orange and pink. A small girl in shiny plastic boots trips over a dog on the pavement. We pass the tennis courts and I am relieved to see that there are two people playing today, hitting the same soggy ball back and forth, laughing at shots that bounce outside the lines which are now barely visible.

We drive past a corrugated bus station and then down a long road, the radio fizzing softly red. I know the road well. Jonathan and I used to come this way when we drove to London, our breath sticky with mint imperials and the exhausts of other cars. He drove always with one hand resting on my leg and when the traffic slowed and the engine began to shudder he would release the clutch and squeeze his hand gently on my thigh and mutter 'third', and I would lean over and adjust the gear-stick.

Suddenly the indicator ticks loudly and Emily winds down her window. Anna turns to me and says, 'We're here.'

We all look at the house. It has a yellow door and off-white window frames and crumbling steps leading up to the entrance. There are net curtains in the downstairs windows and a drooping pot plant on the step. I imagine discarded dentures lying in old tumblers on wicker tables and packets of rusks in the cupboard, and an encrusted toothbrush by the bath. This is all wrong. I do not think of Michael as old. I see him in young men with arms too long for their bodies and hair scruffy against their necks, and then I think of that letter, of Tabitha and of how he did not come back, and then I forget about him. It is easier that way. I refuse to see him in the glassy old men who slouch against bus timetables, or in the musty bowels of Irish pubs. I do not imagine him wearing shapeless cardigans over thin blue shirts, or milkbottle glasses on a string around his neck.

Emily turns off the engine. 'Shall we go inside?'

'I'll stay in the car,' I say abruptly. I am concerned that it would disrupt my cataloguing system entirely if I were to go into the house. Everything would have to be reordered, refiled. I will just sit and watch.

Anna looks at me. 'Really?'

I nod and lean awkwardly back into the seat. Emily and Anna shrug and get out of the car, running up the steps of the house. They look through the windows and the letterbox before opening the front door and going inside.

I am left alone. I lean forward and rest my hand on the gearstick, remembering that lost intimacy I hardly noticed until it was taken away from me. The air in the car is hot and presses down on my chest. I open the door and the rain blows gently onto my cheek, and when I stand up it surprises me that there is no pain in my knees. I walk to the end of the street towards the road with all the buses, and then I turn right and walk a little further. My body feels oddly light. I stop for a moment and stand perfectly still and slot the grooves of my wrinkly fingers into each other, and I wonder what Jonathan would say about all of this.

And that is when I smell it. It is unmistakable, that smell. A light blue, ruffled smell of mashed potatoes and soap, of salty seagulls and shiny whales. Jonathan's smell. I look around to see where it is coming from, almost expecting to see him standing behind me, but there are only cars and a fried chicken shop next to the garage over the road. I lift my nose to the sky and begin to sniff, tentatively at first and then faster and faster until I feel dizzy from too much oxygen and, as I do, I find at last that I can see Jonathan's face as I have not been able to since the day he died. I can see the white hairs on the front of his neck where it slopes into his chest, and his thickly cracked lips and his seaweed eyes. I can see all the bits that don't show up in the glassy photographs that lie dustily in frames on crowded bookshelves that I cannot look at.

It smells of his hand on my shoulder as we walked the streets of Bromley when we were first married. It smells of his fingers twirling the ends of my hair impatiently as I washed the dishes and of his shirt after a limping game of football with Emily in the garden. And it smells of his eyelashes whispering moth-like against my cheek on the last day, kissing me goodbye.

A smell that I never thought to bottle up in an old jam jar and keep in a cool, dark place in case I could never find it again.

The rain has stopped now. I take my notepad from my bag and begin to write in large blotchy letters in case I cannot remember this tomorrow.

And then, when I have finished, I turn and walk back the way I have come, but this time I do not stop. I carry on past Emily's car and up the steps to Michael's front door, and from the hallway I see Anna in the halogen-lit yard at the back of the house, peering upwards through the roof of an empty pigeon-loft and Emily standing next to her, shaking a tin and looking at the sky, and there are newspapers in a pile next to the door and a book left half-open on the arm of a faded green chair. And maybe I am not as practical as I thought.